Sor

Somebody's Luggage

Charles Dickens

with
Charles Allston Collins
Arthur Locker
John Oxenford
Julia Cecilia Stretton

Edited by
Melissa Valiska Gregory
Melisa Klimaszewski

ET REMOTISSIMA PROPE

Hesperus Classics

Hesperus Classics
Published by Hesperus Press Limited
4 Rickett Street, London sw6 1ru
www.hesperuspress.com

Somebody's Luggage first published in *All the Year Round* in 1862
First published by Hesperus Press Limited, 2006

This edition edited by Melissa Valiska Gregory and Melisa Klimaszewski
Introduction and notes © Melissa Valiska Gregory and Melisa Klimaszewski, 2006
Foreword © Philippa Stockley, 2006

Designed and typeset by Fraser Muggeridge studio
Printed in Jordan by the Jordan National Press

isbn: 1-84391-140-x
isbn13: 978-1-84391-140-1

CONTENTS

FOREWORD

If, sitting on the Tube, you open one of the great novels of Charles Dickens, having perhaps not read one since school, beware. Like a ratter, he will have you by the collar with the first sentence; hold you up, snarl, give you a good shake, and keep you for the duration. A writer with no notion of the holding back and spinning out and spreading thin that lamentably so many of us do today, determined that less might really prove more – a philosophy we should never apply to gold, or ice cream. If virtuosity, vigour and range are not enough, the absurdity of Dickens' humour, often from merely meddling with the honest expectations of a blameless sentence, will leave you shaking with laughter:

'What are them things in 24 B?'

So Christopher, the sixty-one-year-old Head Waiter in a nameless London bed-and-dinner establishment, demands of the chambermaid, regarding some items he notices under the bed in a grotty room on the turn of the stairs.

Them things turn out to be Somebody's Luggage, uncollected for many years; and so, deliciously labelled (already there is a hint of parcel tickets, of thin, hard-twisted string and the taste of gum), the 1862 Christmas issue of Charles Dickens' magazine *All the Year Round* takes its portmanteau name and form – a collection of stories by various pens.

Christopher, the unlikely hero, a man born to be a waiter from a long line of waiters, brought up on gin, slops and hopelessness, has risen through the trade into which his mother had unwillingly brought him and out of which his father unwittingly died, to his current impecunious position.

When Christopher notices the dusty luggage and has his equally dusty porter winkle it out (so covered with feathers, he observes, that it might start to lay), he opens, not exactly Pandora's box, but what someone in an expansive mood, prepared to consider that lady-deity's container in the liberal terms of a black portmanteau, a black bag, a desk, a dressing case, a brown paper parcel, a hat box, and an umbrella strapped to a walking stick, might generously compare it with.

Having purchased the luggage from his widow employer (for whose shapely form he nurses admiration), Christopher finds every nook stuffed with writing: in the boots, even between the spokes of the umbrella. 'He was a smeary writer, and wrote a dreadful bad hand. Utterly regardless of ink, he lavished it on every undeserving object…'

Dickens' agility and pleasure in nursing a conceit, however whimsical, is unparalleled, and when Christopher finds that these smoothed-out stories are unnamed, he promptly titles each according to its recent home.

Only a fifty-year-old Dickens, so confident, so absolute, with all his great completed works (except *Our Mutual Friend*) behind him, could harness four writers and cajole or bully them into contributing to this extraordinary collection, each, to all appearances, blithely unaware of what the others wrote. Yet, with his firm hand topping and tailing the event as well as popping up twice in the middle to insinuate a couple of extra stories, the by turns audacious, hilarious, supernatural, or mawkish result will make you read it through again as soon as you have finished.

Yet multiple authorship does come at the inevitable price of a certain patchiness – which even Dickens's two, wonderfully peculiar, insertions cannot quite dispel. In the first, an Englishman has fled to France to try to forget his daughter, whom he has cut off for having an illegitimate child. Instead, M. L'Anglais finds himself forced to reconsider that action when he encounters a young illegitimate girl, Bebelle, who reawakens his compassion.

But the windows of the house of Memory, and the windows of the house of Mercy, are not so easily closed as windows of glass and wood. They fly open unexpectedly; they rattle in the night; they must be nailed up. Mr The Englishman had tried nailing them, but had not driven the nails quite home.

Here is a man who thought he had profitably exchanged love for empty, high-riding principles, but love for a stranger's child leads him back to his daughter. Though hopelessly sentimental, the tale establishes the theme of *Somebody's Luggage*: of losing – and finding.

Dickens' other offering is a masterpiece of oddness. In it, a pavement artist draws superb chalk clichés ('a cherubim… going on a horizontal errand against the wind'), then rents the drawings out to incompetent bodgers who nevertheless guy the public and collect the money – observing which scam drives the artist to fury. Yet, in this angry, deliberately incognito artist, Dickens describes someone who has willingly sold his artistic soul – toadied himself for profit – an offence so grave that punishment is total: the artist loses the girl he is courting, and annihilates himself as thoroughly as he swabs out all traces of his work under cover of dark. In return for betraying his art for money, bitterness is the sole reward.

These stories are not just a collection of parables. One of my favourites is a linked pair, written by Dickens' son-in-law Charles Collins (younger brother of Wilkie). Two years before, Dickens had opposed Collins' marriage with his favourite daughter, Kate; Collins' story relates the triumph of an 'imprudent' marriage over conventional expectation.

In the setting of a great Scottish house party, full of hunting, billiards, and deaf dowagers with cranky dialogue, poor-but-manly Jack Fortescue nobly defers to rich-but-repulsive dandy, Earl Sneyd, over the hand of the most beautiful girl in their circle, Miss Crawcour. Fortescue's bowing-out is commented on by his friend, the narrator, with pithy remarks on the Victorian marriage market – for though Miss Crawcour visibly detests weak, ringleted Sneyd, she is penniless, and must do the best she can: 'I saw… a young girl… about to sacrifice all her happiness, deliberately selling it for money and a coronet… because she was forced into it.'

This so familiar theme of pre-emancipation novels is played out to its dreadful consequence in, for example, Edith Wharton's tragic heroine, Lily Bart in *The House of Mirth*. In Collins' version, perhaps because it is aimed at the Christmas market, there is a qualified triumph. On the brink of throwing away his life in India, since he has thrown away his love (out of what we would consider insane deference to convention), Fortescue is granted a reversal of fortune. Even so, it comes at a horrific price.

But enough of that. What happens to Christopher, the tottering waiter? Poor, untravelled, unloved and thankless, he gains (by means that you must discover yourself) riches, respect, a world view – and, perhaps, a wife.

Spilling out from *Somebody's Luggage* are gingham umbrellas with minds of their own, icebergs steered like ships, and fairy-godmothers hovering on the backs of magical chairs of truth. Opening it, you will wonder (glancing up at your companions on the Tube, with their serious expressions and their white trailing wires) how we all got to be so self-contained, neatly ticketed, and snapped-shut.

– Philippa Stockley, 2006

In the seventh story of *Somebody's Luggage*, 'His Brown Paper Parcel', a talented young artist hires himself out to impostors who pass off his pictures as their own. He grumbles, '[Y]ou think you have seen me. Now, as a safe rule, you have never seen me, and you never will see me. I think that's plainly put – and it's what knocks me over'. Thomas' fate, to be appreciated as an artist but ignored as a person, might be read as Charles Dickens' tongue-in-cheek reflection on the nature of collaborative writing. For *Somebody's Luggage* offers a similar scenario, only in reverse. Instead of several individuals claiming to have accomplished the work of one man, with *Somebody's Luggage*, one man, Dickens, collects the fiction of several friends and fellow writers and publishes the tales under his name. Does Dickens pen the disgruntled Thomas as an expression of his own anxiety about the lack of accreditation the other writers receive, or might he be laughing at his own power to inflict this artist's fate upon others?

To be sure, uncredited authorship was a typical feature of the Victorian periodical press. Following the convention of most journals and newspapers of the period, the individual columns in Dickens' weekly journals, *Household Words* (1850–9) and *All the Year Round* (1859–70), regularly appeared without bylines. There is no evidence to suggest that Dickens deliberately attempted to deceive the public about the collaborative origins of these texts, and the sheer number of them would have made any reader suspicious of a single author who claimed to be so prolific. The special editions of these journals that were issued as Christmas numbers between 1850 and 1867 are no exception. Stopping just short of naming himself as the sole author, Dickens identified himself as the 'conductor', and did not list the contributing authors. Yet he did not go out of his way to publicise the collaborative nature of these pieces, either, despite the emphasis that he placed on their textual nature. In the letter that he sent inviting prospective writers to contribute their work to this 1862 Christmas story, Dickens specified that 'the tales are not supposed to be narrated to any audience, but are supposed to be *in writing*' (our emphasis). Dickens may not have publicised the names of the other authors of this story, but he arranged for the presentation of the individual stories in *Somebody's Luggage* to echo their real-life creation: a collection of texts assembled to create a whole. *Somebody's Luggage* thus stands out as one of the most self-reflexive Christmas numbers, playfully commenting upon both the advantages and troubling consequences of joint authorship.

Somebody's Luggage begins with a bundle of anonymous manuscripts stashed in a stranger's abandoned luggage. Although some of the manuscripts appear, as tradition would dictate, within the writer's discarded desk, most are discovered secreted within more personal compartments, including the author's dressing case, hat box, boots, and even his shaving tackle (although, disappointingly, we never learn exactly what was in the shaving tackle). Nestled next to the intimate articles of the mysterious author's toilette, literally filling his shoes, the manuscripts at once resurrect the actual physical presence of the departed writer and send him packing, so to speak, substituting his fiction for his live body. The idea that one's literary corpus replaces one's corpse resonates, somewhat equivocally, within the context of this collaboratively written text. On one hand, the substitution of text for body supports the idea behind collaborative labour, which reduces an author's monopoly on his or her own work and weakens all claims to individual ownership. In a collaborative project, writers willingly separate their identity from their texts, abandoning their names and leaving only their work behind as loose baggage for someone else to collect. On the other hand, in Dickens' conclusion to *Somebody's Luggage*, the owner of the luggage returns to claim his belongings, only to discover that someone else has already published his stories. While 'Somebody' is thrilled to be in print despite receiving no acknowledgement – not to mention payment – for his work, surely not all authors would be so grateful. Is Dickens meditating on the benefits and limitations of shared authorship? Acknowledging the difficulty of subsuming one's authorial identity but also imagining a fairy-tale reward for those who are willing to do so? In a crescendo of meta-textuality, the manuscripts ultimately appear in print in Dickens' own real-life magazine *All the Year Round*, a happy ending that construes publishing under his name as the ultimate writer's fantasy.

The narrator of Dickens' frame story, a waiter named Christopher, also expresses some ambivalence about the act of collaboration, perhaps because his 'collaborative' actions resemble an act of thievery more than a mutually shared creative process. Christopher may wait tables for a living, but he is a writer at heart. As soon as he discovers the abandoned luggage, he yearns to uncover its mysteries, an obsession he describes with all the florid abandon of a pent-up artist: 'This luggage lay heavy on my mind... [F]rom time to time I stared at it and stared at it, till it seemed to grow big and grow little, and come forward at me and retreat again, and go through all manner of performances resembling intoxication.' He may describe his pen as 'unassuming', but Christopher's sensitive anticipation of his audience's disapproval, followed by his bathetically flattering appeals to his 'fair', 'gentle', and even 'highly intellectual reader', suggests a more sophisticated awareness of his craft. His appropriation of the found manuscripts may be partially dictated by his financial circumstances, but it also offers Christopher a rare opportunity for self-expression, if only by borrowing someone else's words. Christopher's guilt over the author's possible reaction – he 'perspire[s] with the utmost freedom' and even has nightmares when confronted with the manuscripts' original writer – points to the uncomfortable position that collaborative work forces its participants to occupy. Like the author who created him, Christopher at once enables the publication of an unknown writer and steals his identity; the price of public acknowledgement is personal obscurity. As Christopher's readers, moreover, we profit from his theft. Our complicity invites us to question our conventional assumptions about authorial integrity and legitimacy. Who is the author of a collaboratively written piece? Is collaboration nothing more than a form of textual larceny, or a willing surrender of authorial ownership?

Little hard evidence exists to suggest that the other contributors to *Somebody's Luggage*, Charles Collins, Arthur Locker, John Oxenford, and Julia Cecilia Stretton, were excessively bothered by these questions. Far from being resentful, not surprisingly, many Victorian authors were flattered to be invited to participate in Dickens' Christmas numbers. Yet the writers of *Somebody's Luggage* return repeatedly to the twin themes of public authority and recognition, and many of the stories feature characters forced to grapple with their own secondary status in the world at large. Charles Allston Collins' 'His Black Bag' and 'His Writing Desk', for instance, tell the tale of a young soldier whose limited fortune threatens to keep him from marrying his lover. Arthur Locker's 'His Dressing Case' similarly features a lowly sailor who temporarily takes charge of the shipwrecked passengers of an iceberg only to find his authority overturned by the ship's real captain at the end of the tale. 'Poor Tom White!' says the narrator. 'I believe he was a kind-hearted fellow, and well pleased to find that not a single life had been sacrificed… yet I am sure he was sorry to see the captain again'. The description of Tom's mixed emotions – his pleasure at the success of the enterprise combined with his regret at being once more relegated to the status of a minor player – might also describe the feeling of writing a story for (or under) the period's most famous author.

The most extreme portrayal of second-class citizenry occurs in Julia Cecilia Stretton's 'His Portmanteau', continued in 'His Hat Box'. Her tale revolves around the resolutely wimpy Richard Blorage, a man who makes it 'his vocation' to be 'imposed upon'. Bullied by his selfish brother, intimidated by his servants, and hounded by fortune-hunting women, Blorage actually requires supernatural intervention to grow a spine. Stretton's story works to great comic effect, but Dick's refusal to assert himself without divine aid remains oddly disquieting even after he receives his happy ending. Stretton's story serves as a cautionary tale for those individuals who give up too much of themselves.

Perhaps it is important to remember, however, that in subsuming the identities of the other writers under his own, Dickens received blame as well as praise. Although *Somebody's Luggage* sold extremely well, critics disliked the stories that Dickens had not written. This may account for Dickens' decision to omit all but his tales when he republished *Somebody's Luggage* in 1867 as part of a new edition of his work. He even prefaced the volume with the claim that his contributions to the Christmas numbers 'were originally so constructed as that they might express and explain themselves when republished alone', a rather startling renunciation of collaborative writing from a self-described 'conductor' of multiple texts. Indeed, it echoes Christopher's rather lame disavowal of responsibility for the stories he gets into print: 'If there should be any flaw in the writings, or anything missing in the writings, it is Him as is responsible – not me'. Christopher's fear that the collaborative aspect of his text might fail anticipates Dickens' lost faith: they both give up on *Somebody's Luggage*.

What is lost when Dickens abandons his own excess baggage? Without the stories by the other authors, both the entire text of *Somebody's Luggage* and Dickens' individual contributions to it appear less aesthetically remarkable. Contemporary scholars have paid a fair amount of attention to Dickens' 'His Boots' for the light it potentially sheds on his biography, particularly his affair with the young actress Ellen Ternan, whom he met in 1857. Evidence suggests that Dickens visited Ternan in houses that he rented in Boulogne from Ferdinand Beaucourt-Mutuel (1805–81), who serves as a model for M. Mutuel, the story's good-natured Frenchman.[1] Critics rarely recognise, however, that 'His Boots' may have its own literary merits, and examining the story out of context results in a further net loss. The excision of the other contributors dilutes the entire Christmas number, draining it of its tonal richness and regularising the quirky narrative rhythms created by the odd juxtaposition of such a diverse array of texts. It is true that the plot of Dickens' frame story holds together without the internal support of the other writers' tales, but the text becomes livelier, if a little less coherent, when read as a whole. Its eccentric mishmash of tragic melodrama and farce, not to mention good and bad writing, makes for a dynamic reading experience: the more the seams show, the more *Somebody's Luggage* crackles with energy. Even the stories themselves contain sometimes jarring yet intriguing tonal shifts. Charles Allston Collins' two-part story, for example, abruptly jumps from a brilliant satire of the ludicrous nature of aristocratic dinner conversation to a truly awful riding accident. Impressive in their range, the stories that comprise *Somebody's Luggage* are most enjoyable when yoked together as a group. In this Hesperus edition, *Somebody's Luggage* again survives as a complete and enjoyably mismatched set.

– Melissa Valiska Gregory and Melisa Klimaszewski, 2006

1. See Claire Tomalin's *The Invisible Woman* (Penguin, 1991) and John Bowen's 'Bebelle and "His Boots": Dickens, Ellen Ternan and the *Christmas Stories*' in *The Dickensian* 96.3 (Winter 2000): 197–208.

Somebody's Luggage

THE EXTRA CHRISTMAS NUMBER OF ALL THE YEAR ROUND.
CONDUCTED BY CHARLES DICKENS.
CONTAINING THE AMOUNT OF TWO ORDINARY NUMBERS.

CHRISTMAS, 1862

HIS LEAVING IT TILL CALLED FOR
[by Charles Dickens]

The writer of these humble lines being a Waiter, and having come of a family of Waiters, and owning at the present time five brothers who are all Waiters, and likewise an only sister who is a Waitress, would wish to offer a few words respecting his calling; first having the pleasure of hereby in a friendly manner offering the Dedication of the same unto JOSEPH, much respected Head Waiter at the Slamjam Coffee-house, London, E.C., than which a individual more eminently deserving of the name of man, or a more amenable honour to his own head and heart, whether considered in the light of a Waiter or regarded as a human being, do not exist.

In case confusion should arise in the public mind (which it is open to confusion on many subjects) respecting what is meant or implied by the term Waiter, the present humble lines would wish to offer an explanation. It may not be generally known that the person as goes out to wait, is *not* a Waiter. It may not be generally known that the hand as is called in extra, at the Freemasons' Tavern, or the London, or the Albion,[1] or otherwise, is *not* a Waiter. Such hands may be took on for Public Dinners, by the bushel (and you may know them by their breathing with difficulty when in attendance, and taking away the bottle 'ere yet it is half out), but such are *not* Waiters. For, you cannot lay down the tailoring, or the shoemaking, or the brokering, or the green-grocering, or the pictorial periodicalling, or the second-hand wardrobe, or the small fancy, businesses – you cannot lay down those lines of life at your will and pleasure by the half-day or evening, and take up Waitering. You may suppose you can, but you cannot; or you may go so far as to say you do, but you do not. Nor yet can you lay down the gentleman's service when stimulated by prolonged incompatibility on the part of Cooks (and here it may be remarked that Cooking and Incompatibility will be mostly found united), and take up Waitering. It has been ascertained that what a gentleman will sit meek under, at home, he will not bear out of doors, at the Slamjam or any similar establishment. Then, what is the inference to be drawn respecting true Waitering? You must be bred to it. You must be born to it.

Would you know how born to it, Fair Reader – if of the adorable female sex? Then learn from the biographical experience of one that is a Waiter in the sixty-first year of his age.

You were conveyed, ere yet your dawning powers were otherwise developed than to harbour vacancy in your inside – you were conveyed, by surreptitious means, into a pantry adjoining the Admiral Nelson, Civic and General Dining Rooms, there to receive by stealth that healthful sustenance that is the pride and boast of the British female constitution. Your mother was married to your father (himself a distant Waiter) in the profoundest secrecy; for a Waitress known to be married would ruin the best of businesses – it is the same as on the stage. Hence your being smuggled into the pantry, and that – to add to the infliction – by an unwilling grandmother. Under the combined influence of the smells of roast and boiled, and soup, and gas, and malt liquors, you partook of your earliest nourishment; your unwilling grandmother sitting prepared to catch you when your mother was called and dropped you; your grandmother's shawl ever ready to stifle your natural complainings; your innocent mind surrounded by uncongenial cruets, dirty plates, dish covers, and cold gravy; your mother calling down the pipe for veals and porks, instead of soothing you with nursery rhymes. Under these untoward circumstances you were early weaned. Your unwilling grandmother, ever growing more unwilling as your food assimilated less, then contracted habits of shaking you till your system curdled, and your food would not assimilate at all. At length she was no longer spared, and could have been thankfully spared much sooner. When your brothers began to appear in succession, your mother retired, left off her smart dressing (she had previously been a smart dresser), and her dark ringlets (which had previously been flowing), and haunted your father late of nights, lying in wait for him, through all weathers, up the shabby court that led to the back door of the Royal Old Dust-Binn[2] (said to have been so named by George the Fourth), where your father was Head. But the Dust-Binn was going down then, and your father took but little – excepting from a liquid point of view. Your mother's object in those visits was of a housekeeping character, and you was set on to whistle your father out. Sometimes he came out, but generally not. Come or not come, however, all that part of his existence that was unconnected with open Waitering, was kept a close secret, and was acknowledged by your mother to be a close secret, and you and your mother flitted about the court, close secrets both of you, and would scarcely have confessed under torture that you knew your father, or that your father had any name than Dick (which wasn't his name, though he was never known by any other), or that he had kith or kin or chick or child. Perhaps the attraction of this mystery, combined with your father's having a damp compartment to himself, behind a leaky cistern, at the Dust-Binn – a sort of a cellar compartment, with a sink in it, and a smell, and a plate rack and a bottle rack, and three windows that didn't match each other or anything else, and no daylight – caused your young mind to feel convinced that you must grow up to be a Waiter too; but you did feel convinced of it, and so did all your brothers, down to your sister. Every one of you felt convinced that you was born to the Waitering.

At this stage of your career, what was your feelings one day when your father came home to your mother in open broad daylight – of itself an act of Madness on the part of a Waiter – and took to his bed (leastwise, your mother and family's bed), with the statement that his eyes were devilled kidneys. Physicians being in vain, your father expired, after repeating at intervals for a day and a night, when gleams of reason and old business fitfully illuminated his being, 'Two and two is five. And three is sixpence.' Interred in the parochial department of the neighbouring churchyard, and accompanied to the grave by as many Waiters of long standing as could spare the morning time from their soiled glasses (namely, one), your bereaved form was attired in a white neckankecher,[3] and you was took on from motives of benevolence at The George and Gridiron, theatrical and supper. Here, supporting nature on what you found in the plates (which was as it happened, and but too often thoughtlessly immersed in mustard), and on what you found in the glasses (which rarely went beyond driblets and lemon), by night you dropped asleep standing, till you was cuffed awake, and by day was set to polishing every individual article in the coffee room. Your couch being sawdust; your counterpane being ashes of cigars. Here, frequently hiding a heavy heart under the smart tie of your white neckankecher (or correctly speaking lower down and more to the left), you picked up the rudiments of knowledge from an extra, by the name of Bishops, and by calling plate washer, and gradually elevating your mind with chalk on the back of the corner-box partition, until such time as you used the inkstand when it was out of hand, attained to manhood and to be the Waiter that you find yourself.

I could wish here to offer a few respectful words on behalf of the calling so long the calling of myself and family, and the public interest in which is but too often very limited. We are not generally understood. No, we are not. Allowance enough is not made for us. For, say that we ever show a little drooping listlessness of spirits, or what might be termed indifference or apathy. Put it to yourself what would your own state of mind be, if you was one of an enormous family every member of which except you was always greedy, and in a hurry. Put it to yourself that you was regularly replete with animal food at the slack hours of one in the day and again at nine P.M., and that the repleter you was, the more voracious all your fellow creatures came in. Put it to yourself that it was your business when your digestion was well on, to take a personal interest and sympathy in a hundred gentlemen fresh and fresh (say, for the sake of argument, only a hundred), whose imaginations was given up to grease and fat and gravy and melted butter, and abandoned to questioning you about cuts of this, and dishes of that – each of 'em going on as if him and you and the bill of fare was alone in the world. Then look what you are expected to know. You are never out, but they seem to think you regularly attend everywhere. 'What's this, Christopher, that I hear about the smashed Excursion Train?' – 'How are they doing at the Italian Opera, Christopher?' – 'Christopher, what are the real particulars of this business at the Yorkshire Bank?'[4] Similarly a ministry gives me more trouble than it gives the Queen. As to Lord Palmerston,[5] the constant and wearing connection into which I have been brought with his lordship during the last few years, is deserving of a pension. Then look at the Hypocrites we are made, and the lies (white, I hope) that are forced upon us! Why must a sedentary-pursuited Waiter be considered to be a judge of horseflesh, and to have a most tremenjous interest in horse training and racing? Yet it would be half our little incomes out of our pockets if we didn't take on to have those sporting tastes. It is the same (inconceivable why!) with farming. Shooting, equally so. I am sure that so regular as the months of August, September, and October come round, I am ashamed of myself in my own private bosom for the way in which I make believe to care whether or not the grouse is strong on the wing (much their wings or drumsticks either signifies to me, uncooked!), and whether the partridges is plentiful among the turnips, and whether the pheasants is shy or bold, or anything else you please to mention. Yet you may see me, or any other Waiter of my standing, holding on by the back of the box and leaning over a gentleman with his purse out and his bill before him, discussing these points in a confidential tone of voice, as if my happiness in life entirely depended on 'em.

I have mentioned our little incomes. Look at the most unreasonable point of all, and the point on which the greatest injustice is done us! Whether it is owing to our always carrying so much change in our right-hand trousers pocket, and so many halfpence in our coat-tails, or whether it is human nature (which I were loathe to believe), what is meant by the everlasting fable that Head Waiters is rich? How did that fable get into circulation? Who first put it about, and what are the facts to establish the unblushing statement? Come forth, thou slanderer, and refer the public to the Waiter's will in Doctors' Commons[6] supporting thy malignant hiss! Yet this is so commonly dwelt upon – especially by the screws[7] who give Waiters the least – that denial is in vain, and we are obliged, for our credit's sake, to carry our heads as if we were going into a business, when of the two we are much more likely to go into a union.[8] There was formerly a screw as frequented the Slamjam ere yet the present writer had quitted that establishment on a question of tea-ing his assistant staff out of his own pocket, which screw carried the taunt to its bitterest heighth. Never soaring above threepence, and as often as not grovelling on the earth a penny lower, he yet represented the present writer as a large holder of Consols, a lender of money on mortgage, a Capitalist. He has been overheard to dilate to other customers on the allegation that the present waiter put out thousands of pounds at interest, in Distilleries and Breweries. 'Well, Christopher,' he would say (having grovelled his lowest on earth, half a moment before), 'looking out for a House to open, eh? Can't find a business to be disposed of, on a scale as is up to your resources, humph?' To such a dizzy precipice of falsehood has this misrepresentation taken wing, that the well-known and highly respected OLD CHARLES, long eminent at the West Country Hotel, and by some considered the Father of the Waitering, found himself under the obligation to fall into it through so many years that his own wife (for he had an unbeknown old lady in that capacity towards himself) believed it! And what was the consequence? When he was borne to his grave on the shoulders of six picked Waiters, with six more for change, six more acting as pallbearers, all keeping step in a pouring shower without a dry eye visible, and a concourse only inferior to Royalty, his pantry and lodgings was equally ransacked high and low for property and none was found! How could it be found, when, beyond his last monthly collection of walking sticks, umbrellas, and pocket handkerchiefs (which happened to have been not yet disposed of, though he had ever been through life punctual in clearing off his collections by the month), there was no property existing? Such, however, is the force of this universal libel, that the widow of Old Charles, at the present hour an inmate of the Almshouses of the Cork-Cutters' Company, in Blue Anchor-road (identified sitting at the door of one of 'em, in a clean cap and a Windsor armchair, only last Monday), expects John's hoarded wealth to be found hourly! Nay, ere yet he had succumbed to the grisly dart, and when his portrait was painted in oils, life-size, by subscription of the frequenters of the West Country, to hang over the coffee room chimneypiece, there were not wanting those who contended that what is termed the accessories of such portrait ought to be the Bank of England out of window, and a strongbox on the table. And but for better regulated minds contending for a bottle and screw and the attitude of drawing – and carrying their point – it would have been so handed down to posterity.

I am now brought to the title of the present remarks. Having, I hope without offence to any quarter, offered such observations as I felt it my duty to offer, in a free country that has ever dominated the seas, on the general subject, I will now proceed to wait on the particular question.

At a momentous period of my life, when I was off, so far as concerned notice given, with a House that shall be nameless – for the question on which I took my departing stand was a fixed charge for Waiters, and no House as commits itself to that eminently Un-English act of more than foolishness and baseness shall be advertised by me – I repeat, at a momentous crisis when I was off with a House too mean for mention, and not yet on with that to which I have ever since had the honour of being attached in the capacity of Head,[*] I was casting about what to do next. Then it were that proposals were made to me on behalf of my present establishment. Stipulations were necessary on my part, emendations were necessary on my part; in the end, ratifications ensued on both sides, and I entered on a new career.

We are a bed business, and a coffee room business. We are not a general dining business, nor do we wish it. In consequence, when diners drop in, we know what to give 'em as will keep 'em away another time. We are a Private Room or Family business also; but Coffee Room principal. Me and the Directory and the Writing Materials and cetrer[9] occupy a place to ourselves: a place fended off up a step or two at the end of the Coffee Room, in what I call the good old-fashioned style. The good old-fashioned style is, that whatever you want, down to a wafer, you must be olely and solely dependent on the Head Waiter for. You must put yourself a newborn Child into his hands. There is no other way in which a business untinged with Continental Vice can be conducted. (It were bootless to add that if languages is required to be jabbered and English is not good enough, both families and gentlemen had better go somewhere else.)

When I began to settle down in this right-principled and well-conducted House, I noticed under the bed in No. 24 B (which it is up a angle off the staircase, and usually put off upon the lowly minded), a heap of things in a corner. I asked our Head Chambermaid in the course of the day:

'What are them things in 24 B?'

To which she answered with a careless air:

[*] Its name and address at length, with other full particulars, all editorially struck out.

'Somebody's Luggage.'

Regarding her with a eye not free from severity, I says:

'Whose Luggage?'

Evading my eye, she replied:

'Lor! How should *I* know!'

– Being, it may be right to mention, a female of some pertness, though acquainted with her business.

A Head Waiter must be either Head or Tail. He must be at one extremity or the other of the social scale. He cannot be at the waist of it, or anywhere else but the extremities. It is for him to decide which of the extremities.

On the eventful occasion under consideration, I give Mrs Pratchett so distinctly to understand my decision that I broke her spirit as towards myself, then and there, and for good. Let not inconsistency be suspected on account of my mentioning Mrs Pratchett as 'Mrs', and having formerly remarked that a waitress must not be married. Readers are respectfully requested to notice that Mrs Pratchett was not a waitress, but a chambermaid. Now, a chambermaid *may* be married: if Head, generally is married – or says so. It comes to the same thing as expressing what is customary. (N.B. Mr Pratchett is in Australia, and his address there is 'the Bush'.)

Having took Mrs Pratchett down as many pegs as was essential to the future happiness of all parties, I requested her to explain herself.

'For instance,' I says, to give her a little encouragement, 'who is Somebody?'

'I give you my sacred honour, Mr Christopher,' answers Pratchett, 'that I haven't the faintest notion.'

But for the manner in which she settled her cap-strings, I should have doubted this; but in respect of positiveness it was hardly to be discriminated from an affidavit.

'Then you never saw him?' I followed her up with.

'Nor yet,' said Mrs Pratchett, shutting her eyes and making as if she had just took a pill of unusual circumference – which gave a remarkable force to her denial – 'nor yet any servant in this house. All have been changed, Mr Christopher, within five year, and Somebody left his Luggage here before then.'

Enquiry of Miss Martin yielded (in the language of the Bard of A.1.) 'confirmation strong.'[10] So it had really and truly happened. Miss Martin is the young lady at the bar as makes out our bills, and though higher than I could wish, considering her station, is perfectly well behaved.

Further investigations led to the disclosure that there was a bill against this Luggage to the amount of two sixteen six. The Luggage had been lying under the bedstead in 24 B, over six year. The bedstead is a four-poster, with a deal of old hanging and vallance, and is, as I once said, probably connected with more than 24 Bs – which I remember my hearers was pleased to laugh at, at the time.

I don't know why – when DO we know why? – but this Luggage laid heavy on my mind. I fell a wondering about Somebody, and what he had got and been up to. I couldn't satisfy my thoughts why he should leave so much Luggage against so small a bill. For I had the Luggage out within a day or two and turned it over, and the following were the items: – A black portmanteau, a black bag, a desk, a dressing case, a brown paper parcel, a hat box, and an umbrella strapped to a walking stick. It was all very dusty and fluey. I had our porter up to get under the bed and fetch it out, and though he habitually wallows in dust – swims in it from morning to night, and wears a close-fitting waistcoat with black calimanco[11] sleeves for the purpose – it made him sneeze again, and his throat was that hot with it, that it was obliged to be cooled with a drink of Allsopp's draft.[12]

The Luggage so got the better of me, that instead of having it put back when it was well dusted and washed with a wet cloth – previous to which it was so covered with feathers, that you might have thought it was turning into poultry, and would by and by begin to Lay – I say, instead of having it put back, I had it carried into one of my places downstairs. There from time to time I stared at it and stared at it, till it seemed to grow big and grow little, and come forward at me and retreat again, and go through all manner of performances resembling intoxication. When this had lasted weeks – I may say, months, and not be far out – I one day thought of asking Miss Martin for the particulars of the Two sixteen six total. She was so obliging as to extract it from the books – it dating before her time – and here follows a true copy:

Coffee Room.
1856.   No. 4.

		£	s	d
February 2nd.	Pen and paper	0	0	6
	Port Negus	0	2	0
	Ditto	0	2	0
	Pen and paper	0	0	6
	Tumbler broken	0	2	6
	Brandy	0	2	0
	Pen and paper	0	0	6
	Anchovy toast	0	2	6
	Pen and paper	0	0	6
	Bed	0	3	0
February 3rd.	Pen and paper	0	0	6
	Breakfast	0	2	6
	" Broiled ham	0	2	0
	" Eggs	0	1	0
	" Watercresses	0	1	0
	" Shrimps	0	1	0
	Carried forward	£ 1	4	0
	Brought forward	£ 1	4	0
	Pen and paper	0	0	6
	Blotting-paper	0	0	6
	Messenger to Paternoster-row and back	0	1	6
	Again, when No Answer	0	1	6
	Brandy 2s., Devilled Pork chop 2s	0	4	0
	Pens and paper	0	1	0
	Messenger to Albemarle-street and back	0	1	0
	Again (detained), when No Answer	0	1	6
	Saltcellar broken	0	3	6
	Large Liqueur-glass Orange Brandy	0	1	6
	Dinner, Soup Fish Joint and bird	0	7	6
	Bottle old East India Brown	0	8	0
	Pen and paper	0	0	6
		£ 2	16	6

Mem: January 1st, 1857. He went out after dinner, directing Luggage to be ready when he called for it. Never called.

So far from throwing a light upon the subject, this bill appeared to me, if I may so express my doubts, to involve it in a yet more lurid halo. Speculating it over with the Mistress, she informed me that the luggage had been advertised in the Master's time as being to be sold after such and such a day to pay expenses, but no further steps had been taken. (I may here remark that the Mistress is a widow in her fourth year. The Master was possessed of one of those unfortunate constitutions in which Spirits turns to Water, and rises in the ill-starred Victim.)

My speculating it over, not then only but repeatedly, sometimes with the Mistress, sometimes with one, sometimes with another, led up to the Mistress's saying to me – whether at first in joke or in earnest, or half joke and half earnest, it matters not:

'Christopher, I am going to make you a handsome offer.'

(If this should meet her eye – a lovely blue – may she not take it ill my mentioning that if I had been eight or ten year younger, I would have done as much by her! That is, I would have made her *a* offer. It is for others than me to denominate it a handsome one.)

'Christopher, I am going to make you a handsome offer.'

'Put a name to it, ma'am.'

'Look here, Christopher. Run over the articles of Somebody's Luggage. You've got it all by heart, I know.'

'A black portmanteau, ma'am, a black bag, a desk, a dressing case, a brown paper parcel, a hat box, and an umbrella strapped to a walking stick.'

'All just as they were left. Nothing opened, nothing tampered with.'

'You are right, ma'am. All locked but the brown paper parcel, and that sealed.'

The Mistress was leaning on Miss Martin's desk at the bar window, and she taps the open book that lays upon the desk – she has a pretty-made hand, to be sure – and bobs her head over it, and laughs.

'Come,' says she, 'Christopher. Pay me Somebody's bill, and you shall have Somebody's luggage.'

I rather took to the idea from the first moment; but,

'It mayn't be worth the money,' I objected, seeming to hold back.

'That's a Lottery,' says the Mistress, folding her arms upon the book
– it ain't her hands alone that's pretty made: the observation extends
right up her arms – 'Won't you venture two pound sixteen shillings and
sixpence in the Lottery? Why, there's no blanks!' says the Mistress,
laughing and bobbing her head again, 'you *must* win. If you lose, you
must win! All prizes in this Lottery! Draw a blank, and remember,
Gentlemen-Sportsmen, you'll still be entitled to a black portmanteau,
a black bag, a desk, a dressing case, a sheet of brown paper, a hat box,
and an umbrella strapped to a walking stick!'

To make short of it, Miss Martin come round me, and Mrs Pratchett
come round me, and the Mistress she was completely round me already,
and all the women in the house come round me, and if it had been
Sixteen two instead of Two sixteen, I should have thought myself well
out of it. For what can you do when they do come round you?

So I paid the money – down – and such a laughing as there was
among 'em! But I turned the tables on 'em regularly, when I said:

'My family name is Blue Beard. I'm going to open Somebody's
Luggage all alone in the Secret Chamber,[13] and not a female eye catches
sight of the contents!'

Whether I thought proper to have the firmness to keep to this,
don't signify, or whether any female eye, and if any how many, was
really present when the opening of the Luggage came off. Somebody's
Luggage is the question at present: Nobody's eyes, nor yet noses.

What I still look at most, in connection with that Luggage, is the
extraordinary quantity of writing paper, and all written on! And not our
paper neither – not the paper charged in the bill, for we know our paper
– so he must have been always at it. And he had crumpled up this
writing of his, everywhere, in every part and parcel of his luggage.
There was writing in his dressing case, writing in his boots, writing
among his shaving tackle, writing in his hat box, writing folded away
down among the very whalebones of his umbrella.

His clothes wasn't bad, what there was of 'em. His dressing case was
poor – not a particle of silver stopper – bottle apertures with nothing in
'em, like empty little dog kennels – and a most searching description of
tooth powder diffusing itself around, as under a deluded mistake that all

the chinks in the fittings was divisions in teeth. His clothes I parted with, well enough, to a second-hand dealer not far from St. Clement's Danes, in the Strand – him as the officers in the Army mostly dispose of their uniforms to, when hard pressed with debts of honour, if I may judge from their coats and epaulettes diversifying the window, with their backs towards the public. The same party bought in one lot, the portmanteau, the bag, the desk, the dressing case, the hat box, the umbrella, strap, and walking stick. On my remarking that I should have thought those articles not quite in his line, he said: 'No more ith a man'th grandmother, Mithter Chrithtopher; but if any man will bring hith grandmother here, and offer her at a fair trifle below what the'll feth with good luck when the'th thcoured and turned – I'll buy her!'

These transactions brought me home, and, indeed, more than home, for they left a goodish profit on the original investment. And now there remained the writings; and the writings I particular wish to bring under the candid attention of the reader.

I wish to do so without postponement, for this reason. That is to say, namely, viz., i.e., as follows, thus: – Before I proceed to recount the mental sufferings of which I became the prey in consequence of the writings, and before following up that harrowing tale with a statement of the wonderful and impressive catastrophe, as thrilling in its nature as unlooked for in any other capacity, which crowned the ole[14] and filled the cup of unexpectedness to overflowing, the writings themselves ought to stand forth to view. Therefore it is that they now come next. One word to introduce them, and I lay down my pen (I hope, my unassuming pen), until I take it up to trace the gloomy sequel of a mind with something on it.

He was a smeary writer, and wrote a dreadful bad hand. Utterly regardless of ink, he lavished it on every undeserving object – on his clothes, his desk, his hat, the handle of his toothbrush, his umbrella. Ink was found freely on the coffee room carpet by No. 4 table, and two blots was on his restless couch. A reference to the document I have given entire, will show that on the morning of the third of February, eighteen 'fifty-six, he procured his no less than fifth pen and paper. To whatever deplorable act of ungovernable composition he immolated those materials obtained from the bar, there is no doubt that the fatal deed was committed in bed, and that it left its evidences but too plainly, long afterwards, upon the pillowcase.

He had put no Heading to any of his writings. Alas! Was he likely to have a Heading without a Head, and where was *his* Head when he took such things into it! The writings are consequently called, here, by the names of the articles of Luggage to which they was found attached. In some cases, such as his Boots, he would appear to have hid the writings: thereby involving his style in greater obscurity. But his Boots was at least pairs – and no two of his writings can put in any claim to be so regarded.

With a low-spirited anticipation of the gloomy state of mind in which it will be my lot to describe myself as having drooped, when I next resume my artless narrative, I will now withdraw. If there should be any flaw in the writings, or anything missing in the writings, it is Him as is responsible – not me. With that observation in justice to myself, I for the present conclude.

HIS BOOTS
[by Charles Dickens]

'Eh! well then, Monsieur Mutuel! What do I know, what can I say? I assure you that he calls himself Monsieur The Englishman.'

'Pardon. But I think it is impossible,' said M. Mutuel. – A spectacled, snuffy, stooping old gentleman in carpet shoes and a cloth cap with a peaked shade, a loose blue frock coat reaching to his heels, a large limp white shirt frill, and cravat to correspond – that is to say, white was the natural colour of his linen on Sundays, but it toned down with the week.

'It is,' repeated M. Mutuel: his amiable old walnut-shell countenance, very walnut-shelly indeed as he smiled and blinked in the bright morning sunlight, 'it is, my cherished Madame Bouclet, I think, impossible.'

'Hey!' (with a little vexed cry and a great many tosses of her head). 'But it is not impossible that you are a Pig!' retorted Mme Bouclet: a compact little woman of thirty-five or so. 'See then – look there – read! "On the second floor Monsieur L'Anglais." Is it not so?'

'It is so,' said M. Mutuel.

'Good. Continue your morning walk. Get out!' Mme Bouclet dismissed him with a lively snap of her fingers.

The morning walk of M. Mutuel was in the brightest patch that the sun made in the Grande Place of a dull old fortified French town. The manner of his morning walk was with his hands crossed behind him: an umbrella, in figure the express image of himself, always in one hand: a snuffbox in the other. Thus, with the shuffling gait of the Elephant (who really does deal with the very worst trousers maker employed by the Zoological world, and who appeared to have recommended him to M. Mutuel), the old gentleman sunned himself daily when sun was to be had – of course, at the same time sunning a red ribbon[15] at his buttonhole; for was he not an ancient Frenchman?

Being told by one of the angelic sex to continue his morning walk and get out, M. Mutuel laughed a walnut-shell laugh, pulled off his cap at arm's length with the hand that contained his snuffbox, kept it off for a considerable period after he had parted from Mme Bouclet, and continued his morning walk and got out: like a man of gallantry as he was.

The documentary evidence to which Mme Bouclet had referred M. Mutuel, was the list of her lodgers, sweetly written forth by her own Nephew and Bookkeeper, who held the pen of an Angel, and posted up at the side of her gateway for the information of the Police. 'Au second, M. L'Anglais, Proprietaire.' On the second floor, Mr The Englishman, man of property. So it stood; nothing could be plainer.

Madame Bouclet now traced the line with her forefinger, as it were to confirm and settle herself in her parting snap at M. Mutuel, and so, placing her right hand on her hip with a defiant air, as if nothing should ever tempt her to unsnap that snap, strolled out into the Place to glance up at the windows of Mr The Englishman. That worthy happening to be looking out of window at the moment, Mme Bouclet gave him a graceful salutation with her head, looked to the right and looked to the left to account to him for her being there, considered for a moment like one who accounted to herself for somebody she had expected not being there, and re-entered her own gateway. Madame Bouclet let all her house giving on the Place, in furnished flats or floors, and lived up the yard behind, in company with M. Bouclet her husband (great at billiards), an inherited brewing business, several fowls, two carts, a nephew, a little dog in a big kennel, a grapevine, a counting-house, four horses, a married sister (with a share in the brewing business), the husband and two children of the married sister, a parrot, a drum (performed on by the little boy of the married sister), two billeted soldiers, a quantity of pigeons, a fife (played by the nephew in a ravishing manner), several domestics and supernumeraries, a perpetual flavour of coffee and soup, a terrific range of artificial rocks and wooden precipices at least four feet high, a small fountain, and half a dozen large sunflowers.

Now, the Englishman in taking his Appartement – or, as one might say on our side of the Channel, his set of chambers – had given his name, correct to the letter, LANGLEY. But as he had a British way of not opening his mouth very wide on foreign soil, except at meals, the Brewery had been able to make nothing of it but L'Anglais. So, Mr The Englishman he had become and he remained.

'Never saw such a people!' muttered Mr The Englishman, as he now looked out of window. 'Never did, in my life!'

This was true enough, for he had never before been out of his own country – a right little island, a tight little island, a bright little island, a show-fight little island,[16] and full of merit of all sorts; but not the whole round world.

'These chaps,' said Mr The Englishman to himself, as his eye rolled over the Place, sprinkled with military here and there, 'are no more like soldiers –!' Nothing being sufficiently strong for the end of his sentence, he left it unended.

This again (from the point of view of his experience) was strictly correct; for, though there was a great agglomeration of soldiers in the town and neighbouring country, you might have held a grand Review and Field Day[17] of them every one, and looked in vain among them all for a soldier choking behind his foolish stock, or a soldier lamed by his ill-fitting shoes, or a soldier deprived of the use of his limbs by straps and buttons, or a soldier elaborately forced to be self-helpless in all the small affairs of his life. A swarm of brisk bright active bustling handy odd skirmishing fellows, able to turn to cleverly at anything, from a siege to soup, from great guns to needles and thread, from the broadsword exercise to slicing an onion, from making war to making omelettes, was all you would have found.

What a swarm! From the Great Place under the eye of Mr The Englishman, where a few awkward squads from the last conscription were doing the goose-step – some members of those squads still as to their bodies in the chrysalis peasant state of Blouse, and only military butterflies as to their regimentally clothed legs – from the Great Place, away outside the fortifications and away for miles along the dusty roads, soldiers swarmed. All day long, upon the grass-grown ramparts of the town, practising soldiers trumpeted and bugled; all day long, down in angles of dry trenches, practising soldiers drummed and drummed. Every forenoon, soldiers burst out of the great barracks into the sandy gymnasium ground hard by, and flew over the wooden horse, and hung on to flying ropes, and dangled upside down between parallel bars, and shot themselves off wooden platforms, splashes, sparks, coruscations, showers, of soldiers. At every corner of the town wall, every guardhouse, every gateway, every sentry-box, every drawbridge, every reedy ditch and rushy dyke, soldiers soldiers soldiers. And the town being pretty well all wall, guardhouse, gateway, sentry-box, drawbridge, reedy ditch and rushy dyke, the town was pretty well all soldiers.

What would the sleepy old town have been without the soldiers, seeing that even with them it had so overslept itself as to have slept its echoes hoarse, its defensive bars and locks and bolts and chains all rusty, and its ditches stagnant! From the days when VAUBAN[18] engineered it to that perplexing extent that to look at it was like being knocked on the head with it: the stranger becoming stunned and stertorous under the shock of its incomprehensibility – from the days when VAUBAN made it the express incorporation of every substantive and adjective in the art of military engineering, and not only twisted you into it and twisted you out of it, to the right, to the left, opposite, under here, over there, in the dark, in the dirt, by gateway, archway, covered way, dry way, wet way, fosse, portcullis, drawbridge, sluice, squat tower, pierced wall, and heavy battery, but likewise took a fortifying dive under the neighbouring country, and came to the surface three or four miles off, blowing out incomprehensible mounds and batteries among the quiet crops of chicory and beetroot – from those days to these, the town had been asleep, and dust and rust and must had settled on its drowsy Arsenals and Magazines, and grass had grown up in its silent streets.

On market days alone, its Great Place suddenly leaped out of bed. On market days, some friendly enchanter struck his staff upon the stones of the Great Place, and instantly arose the liveliest booths and stalls and sittings and standings, and a pleasant hum of chaffering and huckstering from many hundreds of tongues, and a pleasant though peculiar blending of colours – white caps, blue blouses, and green vegetables – and at last the Knight destined for the adventure seemed to have come in earnest, and all the Vaubanois sprang up awake. And now, by long low-lying avenues of trees, jolting in white-hooded donkey cart, and on donkey back, and in tumbril and waggon and cart and cabriolet, and afoot with barrow and burden – and along the dykes and ditches and canals, in little peak-prowed country boats – came peasant men and women in flocks and crowds, bringing articles for sale. And here you had boots and shoes and sweetmeats and stuffs to wear, and here (in the cool shade of the Town Hall) you had milk and cream and butter and cheese, and here you had fruits and onions and carrots and all things needful for your soup, and here you had poultry and flowers and protesting pigs, and here new shovels axes spades and bill-hooks for your farming work, and here huge mounds of bread, and here your unground grain in sacks, and here your children's dolls, and here the cake seller announcing his wares by beat and roll of drum. And hark! fanfaronade of trumpets, and here into the Great Place, resplendent in an open carriage with four gorgeously attired servitors up behind, playing horns drums and cymbals, rolled 'the Daughter of a Physician' in massive golden chains and earrings, and blue-feathered hat, shaded from the admiring sun by two immense umbrellas of artificial roses, to dispense (from motives of philanthropy) that small and pleasant dose that had cured so many thousands! Toothache earache headache heartache stomachache debility nervousness fits faintings fever ague, all equally cured by the small and pleasant dose of the great Physician's great daughter! The process was this: – she, the Daughter of a Physician, proprietress of the superb equipage you now admired, with its confirmatory blasts of trumpet drum and cymbal, told you so: – On the first day after taking the small and pleasant dose, you would feel no particular influence beyond a most harmonious sensation of indescribable and irresistible joy; on the second day, you would be so astonishingly better that you would think yourself changed into somebody else; on the third day, you would be entirely free from your disorder, whatever its nature and however long you had had it, and would seek out the Physician's daughter, to throw yourself at her feet, kiss the hem of her garment, and buy as many more of the small and pleasant doses as by the sale of all your few effects you could obtain; but she would be inaccessible – gone for herbs to the Pyramids of Egypt – and you would be (though cured) reduced to despair! Thus would the Physician's daughter drive her trade (and briskly too), and thus would the buying and selling and mingling of tongues and colours continue until the changing sunlight, leaving the Physician's daughter in the shadow of high roofs, admonished her to jolt out westward, with a departing effect of gleam and glitter on the splendid equipage and brazen blast. And now the enchanter struck his staff upon the stones of the Great Place once more, and down went the booths the sittings and standings, and vanished the merchandise, and with it the barrows donkeys, donkey carts and tumbrils and all other things on wheels and feet, except the slow scavengers with unwieldy carts and meagre horses, clearing up the rubbish, assisted by the sleek town pigeons, better plumped out than on non-market days. While there was yet an hour or two to wane before the autumn sunset, the loiterer outside town gate and drawbridge and postern and double-ditch, would see the last white-hooded cart lessening in the avenue of lengthening shadows of trees, or the last country boat, paddled by the last market woman on her way home, showing black upon the reddening long low narrow dyke between him and the mill; and as the paddle-parted scum and weed closed over the boat's track, he might be comfortably sure that its sluggish rest would be trouble no more until next market day.

As it was not one of the Great Place's days for getting out of bed when Mr The Englishman looked down at the young soldiers practising the goose-step there, his mind was left at liberty to take a military turn.

'These fellows are billeted everywhere about,' said he, 'and to see them lighting the people's fires, boiling the people's pots, minding the people's babies, rocking the people's cradles, washing the people's greens, and making themselves generally useful, in every sort of un-military way, is most ridiculous! – Never saw such a set of fellows; never did in my life!'

All perfectly true again. Was there not Private Valentine, in that very house, acting as sole housemaid, valet, cook, steward, and nurse, in the family of his captain, M. le Capitaine De la Cour – cleaning the floors, making the beds, doing the marketing, dressing the captain, dressing the dinners, dressing the salads, and dressing the baby, all with equal readiness? Or, to put him aside, he being in loyal attendance on his Chief, was there not Private Hyppolite, billeted at the Perfumer's two hundred yards off, who, when not on duty, volunteered to keep shop while the fair Perfumeress stepped out to speak to a neighbour or so, and laughingly sold soap with his war sword girded on him? Was there not Emile, billeted at the Clockmaker's, perpetually turning to of an evening with his coat off, winding up the stock? Was there not Eugène, billeted at the Tinman's, cultivating, pipe in mouth, a garden four feet square for the tinman, in the little court behind the shop, and extorting the fruits of the earth from the same, on his knees, with the sweat of his brow? Not to multiply examples, was there not Baptiste, billeted on the poor Water Carrier, at that very instant sitting on the pavement in the sunlight, with his martial legs asunder, and one of the Water Carrier's spare pails between them, which (to the delight and glory of the heart of the Water Carrier coming across the Place from the fountain, yoked and burdened) he was painting bright green outside and bright red within? Or, to go no further than the Barber's at the very next door, was there not Corporal Théophile –

'No,' said Mr The Englishman, glancing down at the Barber's, 'he is not there at present. There's the child though.'

A mere mite of a girl stood on the steps of the Barber's shop, looking across the Place. A mere baby, one might call her, dressed in the close white linen cap that small French country children wear (like the Children in Dutch pictures), and in a frock of homespun blue, which had no shape except where it was tied round her little fat throat. So that, being naturally short and round all over, she looked, behind, as if she had been cut off at her natural waist, and had had her head neatly fitted on it.

'There's the child though.'

To judge from the way in which the dimpled hand was rubbing the eyes, the eyes had been closed in a nap and were newly opened. But they seemed to be looking so intently across the Place, that the Englishman looked in the same direction.

'Oh!' said he, presently, 'I thought as much. The Corporal's there.'

The Corporal, a smart figure of a man of thirty: perhaps a thought under the middle size, but very neatly made – a sunburnt Corporal with a brown peaked beard – faced about at the moment, addressing voluble words of instruction to the squad in hand. Nothing was amiss or awry about the Corporal. A lithe and nimble Corporal, quite complete, from the sparkling dark eyes under his knowing uniform cap, to his sparkling white gaiters. The very image and presentment of a Corporal of his country's army, in the line of his shoulders, the line of his waist, the broadest line of his Bloomer trousers, and their narrowest line at the calf of his leg.

Mr The Englishman looked on, and the child looked on, and the Corporal looked on (but the last-named at his men), until the drill ended a few minutes afterwards and the military sprinkling dried up directly and was gone. Then said Mr The Englishman to himself, 'Look here! By George!' And the Corporal, dancing towards the Barber's with his arms wide open, caught up the child, held her over his head in a flying attitude, caught her down again, kissed her, and made off with her into the Barber's house.

Now, Mr The Englishman had had a quarrel with his erring and disobedient and disowned daughter, and there was a child in that case too. Had not his daughter been a child, and had she not taken angel flights above his head as this child had flown above the Corporal's?

'He's a' – National Participled[19] – 'fool!' said the Englishman. And shut his window.

But the windows of the house of Memory, and the windows of the house of Mercy, are not so easily closed as windows of glass and wood. They fly open unexpectedly; they rattle in the night; they must be nailed up. Mr The Englishman had tried nailing them, but had not driven the nails quite home. So he passed but a disturbed evening and a worse night.

By nature a good-tempered man? No; very little gentleness, confounding the quality with weakness. Fierce and wrathful when crossed? Very, and stupendously unreasonable. Moody? Exceedingly so. Vindictive? Well, he *had* had scowling thoughts that he would formally curse his daughter, as he had seen it done on the stage. But remembering that the real Heaven is some paces removed from the mock one in the great chandelier of the Theatre, he had given that up.

And he had come abroad to be rid of his repudiated daughter for the rest of his life. And here he was.

At bottom, it was for this reason more than for any other that Mr The Englishman took it extremely ill that Corporal Théophile should be so devoted to little Bebelle, the child at the Barber's shop. In an unlucky moment he had chanced to say to himself, 'Why, confound the fellow, he is not her father!' There was a sharp sting in the speech that ran into him suddenly and put him in a worse mood. So he had National

Participled the unconscious Corporal with most hearty emphasis, and had made up his mind to think no more about such a mountebank.[20]

But, it came to pass that the Corporal was not to be dismissed. If he had known the most delicate fibres of the Englishman's mind, instead of nothing knowing on earth about him, and if he had been the most obstinate Corporal in the Grand Army of France instead of being the most obliging, he could not have planted himself with more determined immovability plump in the midst of all the Englishman's thoughts. Not only so, but he seemed to be always in his view. Mr The Englishman had but to look out of window, to look upon the Corporal with Little Bebelle. He had but to go for a walk, and there was the Corporal walking with Bebelle. He had but to come home again, disgusted, and the Corporal and Bebelle were at home before him. If he looked out at his back windows early in the morning, the Corporal was in the barber's back-yard, washing and dressing and brushing Bebelle. If he took refuge at his front windows, the Corporal brought his breakfast out into the Place, and shared it there with Bebelle. Always Corporal and always Bebelle. Never Corporal without Bebelle. Never Bebelle without Corporal.

Mr The Englishman was not particularly strong in the French language as a means of oral communication, though he read it very well. It is with languages as with people – when you only know them by sight, you are apt to mistake them; you must be on speaking terms before you can be said to have established an acquaintance.

For this reason, Mr The Englishman had to gird up his loins considerably, before he could bring himself to the point of exchanging ideas with Mme Bouclet on the subject of this Corporal and this Bebelle. But Mme Bouclet looking in apologetically one morning to remark, that O Heaven she was in a state of desolation because the lampmaker had not sent home that lamp confided to him to repair, but that truly he was a lampmaker against whom the whole world shrieked out, Mr The Englishman seized the occasion.

'Madame, that baby – '

'Pardon, monsieur. That lamp.'

'No, no, that little girl.'

'But, pardon!' said Mme Bouclet, angling for a clue; 'one cannot light a little girl, or send her to be repaired?'

'The little girl – at the house of the barber.'

'Ah-h-h!' cried Mme Bouclet, suddenly catching the idea, with her delicate little line and rod. 'Little Bebelle? Yes, yes, yes! And her friend the Corporal? Yes, yes, yes, yes! So genteel of him; is it not?'

'He is not – ?'

'Not at all; not at all! He is not one of her relations. Not at all!'

'Why then, he – '

'Perfectly!' cried Mme Bouclet, 'you are right, monsieur. It is so genteel of him. The less relation, the more genteel. As you say.'

'Is she – ?'

'The child of the barber?' Mme Bouclet whisked up her skillful little line and rod again. 'Not at all, not at all! She is the child of – in a word, of no one.'

'The wife of the barber, then – ?'

'Indubitably. As you say. The wife of the barber receives a small stipend to take care of her. So much by the month. Eh, then! It is without doubt very little, for we are all poor here.'

'You are not poor, madame.'

'As to my lodgers,' replied Mme Bouclet, with a smiling and a gracious bend of her head, 'no. As to all things else, so-so.'

'You flatter me, madame.'

'Monsieur, it is you who flatter me in living here.'

Certain fishy gasps on Mr The Englishman's part, denoting that he was about to resume his subject under difficulties, Mme Bouclet observed him closely, and whisked up her delicate line and rod again with triumphant success.

'Oh no, monsieur, certainly not. The wife of the barber is not cruel to the poor child, but she is careless. Her health is delicate, and she sits all day, looking out at window. Consequently, when the Corporal first came, the poor little Bebelle was much neglected.'

'It is a curious – ' began Mr The Englishman.

'Name? That Bebelle? Again, you are right, monsieur. But it is a playful name for Gabrielle.'

'And so the child is a mere fancy of the Corporal's?' said Mr The Englishman, in a gruffly disparaging tone of voice.

'Eh well!' returned Mme Bouclet, with a pleading shrug: 'one must love something. Human nature is weak.'

('Devilish weak,' muttered the Englishman in his own language.)

'And the Corporal,' pursued Mme Bouclet, 'being billeted at the barber's – where he will probably remain a long time, for he is attached to the General – and finding the poor unowned child in need of being loved, and finding himself in need of loving – why, there you have it all, you see!'

Mr The Englishman accepted this interpretation of the matter with an indifferent grace, and observed to himself, in an injured manner, when he was again alone: 'I shouldn't mind it so much, if these people were not such a' – National Participled – 'sentimental people!'

There was a Cemetery outside the town, and it happened ill for the reputation of the Vaubanois in this sentimental connection, that he took a walk there that same afternoon. To be sure there were some wonderful things in it (from the Englishman's point of view), and of a certainty in all Britain you would have found nothing like it. Not to mention the fanciful flourishes of hearts and crosses, in wood and iron, that were planted all over the place, making it look very like a Firework ground where a most splendid pyrotechnic display might be expected after dark, there were so many wreaths upon the graves, embroidered, as it might be, 'To my mother,' 'To my daughter,' 'To my father,' 'To my brother,' 'To my sister,' 'To my friend,' and those many wreaths were in so many stages of elaboration and decay, from the wreath of yesterday all fresh colour and bright beads, to the wreath of last year, a poor mouldering wisp of straw! There were so many little gardens and grottos made upon graves, in so many tastes, with plants and shells and plaster figures and porcelain pitchers, and so many odds and ends! There were so many tributes of remembrance hanging up, not to be discriminated by the closest inspection from little round waiters, whereon were depicted in glowing hues either a lady or a gentleman with a white pocket handkerchief out of all proportion, leaning, in a state of the most faultless mourning and most profound affliction, on the most architectural and gorgeous urn! There were so many surviving wives who had put their names on the tombs of their deceased husbands with a blank for the date of their own departure from this weary world; and there were so many surviving husbands who had rendered the same homage to their deceased wives; and out of the number there must have been so many who had long ago married again! In fine, there was so much in the place that would have seemed mere frippery to a stranger, save for the consideration that the lightest paper flower that lay upon the poorest heap of earth was never touched by a rude hand, but perished there, a sacred thing.

'Nothing of the solemnity of Death, here,' Mr The Englishman had been going to say; when this last consideration touched him with a mild appeal, and on the whole he walked out without saying it. 'But these people are,' he insisted, by way of compensation when he was well outside the gate, 'they are so,' Participled, 'sentimental!'

His way back lay by the military gymnasium ground. And there he passed the Corporal glibly instructing young soldiers how to swing themselves over rapid and deep watercourses on their way to Glory, by means of a rope, and himself deftly plunging off a platform and flying a hundred feet or two as an encouragement to them to begin. And there he also passed, perched on a crowning eminence (probably by the Corporal's careful hands), the small Bebelle, with her round eyes wide open, surveying the proceeding like a wondering sort of blue and white bird.

'If that child was to die;' this was his reflection as he turned his back and went his way, ' – and it would almost serve the fellow right for making such a fool of himself – I suppose we should have *him* sticking up a wreath and a waiter in that fantastic burying ground.'

Nevertheless, after another early morning or two of looking out of window, he strolled down into the Place, when the Corporal and Bebelle were walking there, and touching his hat to the Corporal (an immense achievement) wished him Good Day.

'Good day, monsieur.'

'This is a rather pretty child you have here,' said Mr The Englishman, taking her chin in his hand, and looking down into her astonished blue eyes.

'Monsieur, she is a very pretty child,' returned the Corporal, with a stress on his polite correction of the phrase.

'And good?' said The Englishman.

'And very good. Poor little thing!'

'Hah!' The Englishman stooped down and patted her cheek: not without awkwardness, as if he were going too far in his conciliation. 'And what is this medal round your neck, my little one?'

Bebelle having no other reply on her lips than her chubby right fist, the Corporal offered his services as interpreter.

'Monsieur demands, what is this, Bebelle?'

'It is the Holy Virgin,' said Bebelle.

'And who gave it you?' asked The Englishman.

'Théophile.'

'And who is Théophile?'

Bebelle broke into a laugh, laughed merrily and heartily, clapped her chubby hands, and beat her little feet on the stone pavement of the Place.

'He doesn't know Théophile! Why he doesn't know anyone! He doesn't know anything!' Then, sensible of a small solecism in her manners, Bebelle twisted her right hand in a leg of the Corporal's Bloomer trousers, and laying her cheek against the place, kissed it.

'Monsieur Théophile, I believe?' said The Englishman to the Corporal.

'It is I, monsieur.'

'Permit me.' Mr The Englishman shook him heartily by the hand and turned away. But he took it mighty ill that old M. Mutuel in his patch of sunlight, upon whom he came as he turned, should pull off his cap to him with a look of pleased approval. And he muttered, in his own tongue, as he returned the salutation, 'Well, walnut-shell! And what business is it of *yours*?'

Mr The Englishman went on for many weeks passing but disturbed evenings and worse nights, and constantly experiencing that those aforesaid windows in the houses of Memory and Mercy rattled after dark, and that he had very imperfectly nailed them up. Likewise, he went on for many weeks, daily improving the acquaintance of the Corporal and Bebelle. That is to say, he took Bebelle by the chin, and the Corporal by the hand, and offered Bebelle sous and the Corporal cigars, and even got the length of changing pipes with the Corporal and kissing Bebelle. But he did it all in a shamefaced way, and always took it extremely ill that M. Mutuel in his patch of sunlight should note what he did. Whenever that seemed to be the case, he always growled in his own tongue, 'There you are again, walnut-shell! What business is it of *yours?*'

In a word, it had become the occupation of Mr The Englishman's life to look after the Corporal and little Bebelle, and to resent old M. Mutuel's looking after *him*. An occupation only varied by a fire in the town one windy night, and much passing of water buckets from hand to hand (in which the Englishman rendered good service), and much beating of drums – when all of a sudden the Corporal disappeared.

Next, all of a sudden, Bebelle disappeared.

She had been visible a few days later than the Corporal – sadly deteriorated as to washing and brushing – but she had not spoken when addressed by Mr The Englishman, and had looked scared and had run away. And now it would seem that she had run away for good. And there lay the Great Place under the windows, bare and barren.

In his shamefaced and constrained way, Mr The Englishman asked no question of anyone, but watched from his front windows, and watched from his back windows, and lingered about the Place, and peeped in at the Barber's shop, and did all this and much more with a whistling and tune-humming pretence of not missing anything, until one afternoon when M. Mutuel's patch of sunlight was in shadow, and when according to all rule and precedent he had no right whatever to bring his red ribbon out of doors, behold here he was, advancing with his cap already in his hand twelve paces off!

Mr The Englishman had got as far into his usual objurgation as 'What bu-si-' when he checked himself.

'Ah, it is sad, it is sad! Helas, it is unhappy, it is sad!' Thus, old M. Mutuel, shaking his grey head.

'What busin- at least, I would say what do you mean, Monsieur Mutuel?'

'Our Corporal. Helas, our dear Corporal!'

'What has happened to him?'

'You have not heard?'

'No.'

'At the fire. But he was so brave, so ready. Ah, too brave, too ready!'

'May the devil carry you away,' the Englishman broke in impatiently; 'I beg your pardon – I mean me – I am not accustomed to speak French – go on, will you!'

'And a falling beam – '

'Good God!' exclaimed the Englishman. 'It was a private soldier who was killed?'

'No. A Corporal, the same Corporal, our dear Corporal. Beloved by all his comrades. The funeral ceremony was touching – penetrating. Monsieur The Englishman, your eyes fill with tears.'

'What bu-si-'

'Monsieur The Englishman, I honour those emotions. I salute you with profound respect. I will not obtrude myself upon your noble heart.'

Monsieur Mutuel, a gentleman in every thread of his cloudy linen, under whose wrinkled hand every grain in the quarter of an ounce of poor snuff in his poor little tin box became a gentleman's property – M. Mutuel passed on with his cap in his hand.

'I little thought,' said the Englishman, after walking for several minutes, and more than once blowing his nose, 'when I was looking round that Cemetery – I'll go there!'

Straight he went there, and when he came within the gate he paused, considering whether he should ask at the lodge for some direction to the grave. But he was less than ever in a mood for asking questions, and he thought, 'I shall see something on it, to know it by.'

In search of the Corporal's grave, he went softly on, up this walk and down that, peering in among the crosses and hearts and columns and obelisks and tombstones for a recently disturbed spot. It troubled him now, to think how many dead there were in the cemetery – he had not thought them a tenth part so numerous before – and, after he had walked and sought for some time, he said to himself as he struck down a new vista of tombs, 'I might suppose that everyone was dead but I.'

Not everyone. A live child was lying on the ground asleep. Truly he had found something on the Corporal's grave to know it by, and the something was Bebelle.

With such a loving will had the dead soldier's comrades worked at his resting place, that it was already a neat garden. On the green turf of the garden, Bebelle lay sleeping, with her cheek touching it. A plain unpainted little wooden Cross was planted in the turf, and her short arm embraced this little Cross, as it had many a time embraced the Corporal's neck. They had put a tiny flag (the flag of France) at his head, and a laurel garland.

Mr The Englishman took off his hat, and stood for a while silent. Then, covering his head again, he bent down on one knee, and softly roused the child.

'Bebelle! My little one!'

Opening her eyes, on which the tears were still wet, Bebelle was at first frightened; but seeing who it was, she suffered him to take her in his arms, looking steadfastly at him.

'You must not lie here my little one. You must come with me.'

'No, no. I can't leave Théophile. I want the good dear Théophile.'

'We will go and seek him, Bebelle. We will go and look for him in England. We will go and look for him at my daughter's, Bebelle.'

'Shall we find him there?'

'We shall find the best part of him there. Come with me, poor forlorn little one. Heaven is my witness,' said the Englishman, in a low voice, as, before he rose, he touched the turf above the gentle Corporal's breast, 'that I thankfully accept this trust!'

It was a long way for the child to have come unaided. She was soon asleep again, with her embrace transferred to the Englishman's neck. He looked at her worn shoes, and her galled feet, and her tired face, and believed that she had come there every day.

He was leaving the grave with the slumbering Bebelle in his arms, when he stopped, looked wistfully down at it, and looked wistfully at the other graves around. 'It is the innocent custom of the people,' said Mr The Englishman, with hesitation, 'I think I should like to do it. No one sees.'

Careful not to wake Bebelle as he went, he repaired to the lodge where such little tokens of remembrance were sold, and bought two wreaths. One, blue and white and glistening silver, 'To my friend;' one of a soberer red and black and yellow, 'To my friend.' With these he went back to the grave, and so down on one knee again. Touching the child's lips with the brighter wreath, he guided her hand to hang it on the Cross; then hung his own wreath there. After all, the wreaths were not far out of keeping with the little garden. To my friend. To my friend.

Mr The Englishman took it very ill when he looked round a street corner into the Great Place, carrying Bebelle in his arms, that old Mutuel should be there airing his red ribbon. He took a world of pains to dodge the worthy Mutuel, and devoted a surprising amount of time and trouble to skulking into his own lodging like a man pursued by Justice. Safely arrived there at last, he made Bebelle's toilette with as accurate a remembrance as he could bring to bear upon that work, of the way in which he had often seen the poor Corporal make it, and, having given her to eat and drink, laid her down on his own bed. Then, he slipped out into the barber's shop, and after a brief interview with the barber's wife and a brief recourse to his purse and card case, came back again, with the whole of Bebelle's personal property in such a very little bundle that it was quite lost under his arm.

As it was irreconcilable with his whole course and character that he should carry Bebelle off in state, or receive any compliments or congratulations on that feat, he devoted the next day to getting his two portmanteaus out of the house by artfulness and stealth, and to comporting himself in every particular as if he were going to run away – except indeed that he paid his few debts in the town, and prepared a letter to leave for Mme Bouclet, enclosing a sufficient sum of money in lieu of notice. A railway train would come through at midnight, and by that train he would take away Bebelle to look for Théophile in England and at his forgiven daughter's.

At midnight on a moonlight night, Mr The Englishman came creeping forth like a harmless assassin, with Bebelle on his breast instead of a dagger. Quiet the Great Place, and quiet the never-stirring streets; closed the cafés; huddled together motionless their billiard balls; drowsy the guard or sentinel on duty here and there; lulled, for the time, by sleep, even the insatiate appetite of the Office of Town-dues.

Mr The Englishman left the Place behind and left the streets behind, and left the civilian-inhabited town behind, and descended down among the military works of Vauban, hemming all in. As the shadow of the first heavy arch and postern fell upon him and was left behind, as the shadow of the second heavy arch and postern fell upon him and was left behind, as his hollow tramp over the first drawbridge was succeeded by a gentler sound, as his hollow tramp over the second drawbridge was succeeded by a gentler sound, as he overcame the stagnant ditches one by one, and passed out where the flowing waters were and where the moonlight, so the dark shades and the hollow sounds and the unwholesomely locked currents of his soul, were vanquished and set free. See to it, Vaubans, of your own hearts, who gird them in with triple walls and ditches, and with bolt and chain and bar and lifted bridge – raze those fortifications and lay them level with the all-absorbing dust, before the night cometh when no hand can work!

All went prosperously, and he got into an empty carriage in the train, where he could lay Bebelle on the seat over against him, as on a couch, and cover her from head to foot with his mantle. He had just drawn himself up from perfecting this arrangement, and had just leaned back in his own seat contemplating it with great satisfaction, when he became aware of a curious appearance at the open carriage window – a ghostly little tin box floating up in the moonlight, and hovering there.

He leaned forward and put out his head. Down among the rails and wheels and ashes, M. Mutuel, red ribbon and all!

'Excuse me, Monsieur The Englishman,' said M. Mutuel, holding up his box at arm's length, the carriage being so high and he so low, 'but I shall reverence the little box forever, if your so generous hand will take a pinch from it at parting.'

Mr The Englishman reached out of the window before complying, and – without asking the old fellow what business it was of his – shook hands and said, 'Adieu! God bless you!'

'And Mr The Englishman, God bless *you*!' cried Mme Bouclet, who was also there among the rails and wheels and ashes. 'And God will bless you in the happiness of the protected child now with you. And God will bless you in your child at home. And God will bless you in your own remembrances. And this from me!'

He had barely time to catch a bouquet from her hand, when the train was flying through the night. Round the paper that enfolded it was bravely written (doubtless by the nephew who held the pen of an Angel), 'Homage to the friend of the friendless.'

'Not bad people, Bebelle!' said Mr The Englishman, softly drawing the mantle a little from her sleeping face, that he might kiss it, 'though they are so – '

Too 'sentimental' himself at the moment to be able to get out that word, he added nothing but a sob, and travelled for some miles, through the moonlight, with his hand before his eyes.

HIS UMBRELLA
[by John Oxenford]

It was not in the spirit of officious gallantry that I put my best foot forward, in order to overtake the lady who was walking a few yards before me, across the large field that adjoins the pretty village of Ivyton. About the attractive qualities of her face and figure I did not care a straw, but she carried one potent charm about her that had for me a fascination wholly irresistible – she carried an umbrella. That the potency of this charm may be fully appreciated, I ought to state that the rain was falling in torrents, and that, although it was early in the year, I was not only without an umbrella, but was also destitute of an over-coat: having carelessly left one of those useful habiliments in the railway carriage. The shades of evening were just deepening into night, and I need not explain that the sensation of being drenched through by a rain that one can scarcely see, is infinitely more disagreeable than the attack of a shower in broad daylight. To the eye the appearance of rapidly falling rain is rather lively than otherwise, and to some extent counteracts the annoyance of a wetting. But in being made aware of the presence of moisture by the sense of feeling alone there is something incalculably dismal and desolate.

There was hope in that umbrella (a gingham umbrella). Surely, under the circumstances, I could solicit a share in it without being deemed extremely rude and impertinent. I slushed my way through the interminable field, and gained upon the figure. Its outline I could plainly distinguish. It was certainly a female, the dress was of a light colour, and – most important particular – the wearer of the dress carried, as I have said, a very large umbrella – a gingham umbrella. More I could not ascertain, save that the object of my pursuit was endowed with a less amount of curiosity than is usually ascribed to the fair sex. As my feet often glided from the slippery path, and splashed into the small puddles by which in many places it was burdened, the noise I made must have been considerable; and most people are anxious to know what sort of a person is walking behind them, when they are in a field about nightfall. Such, however, was not the case with the lady before me. Armed with her umbrella against the inclemencies of the weather, she seemed regardless of everything else.

As I have said, I gained upon the lady; but even when I was at her side, with my head under her umbrella (I believe I have already described it as a gingham umbrella), she made no effort to see me or to avoid me. Apparently looking straight before her, she went on as at first; and it is worthy of remark, that whereas I made a little splash at almost every step, she seemed to pick her way without difficulty. The few courteous words I uttered, did not seem to reach her ear. Perhaps she was deaf? On this supposition, I gently took the gingham umbrella by the handle, politely intending to carry it in such a way as to confer upon her the largest share of its benefits. She made no resistance, but let it go at once, and, what was very strange, no sooner was it safely in my grasp, than I found myself alone! Yes, no one was beside me; there I stood, whole and sole master of a gingham umbrella. Dressed as she was in light raiment, the lady, however rapidly she might have run away, ought to have been visible in some direction; but she was not visible in any direction.

How wrong it is to form hasty judgments. Five minutes before, I had settled in my own mind that the umbrella was the engrossing object of the lady's thoughts. Now, I could clearly see that she did not value it to the extent of a single clutch. If she had merely wanted to be freed from me, she might have gone with the umbrella in her hand, for I did not hold it so very tight. Perhaps the umbrella was more objectionable than myself, and she was glad to get rid of it? The rain that rattled on the silk seemed anxious to demonstrate the utter fallacy of this hypothesis.

I felt comfortable enough in the parlour of the Jolly Navigators, sipping my glass of hot brandy and water as a preventive against the ill effects of the wetting, smoking my cigar, and idly watching my – let me rather say *the* – umbrella, as it lay open before the fire. The inn was close to the station, and I by no means regretted that at least half an hour would elapse before the arrival of the train that was to convey me back to town. Literally doing nothing, I was ready to take an interest in anything, and was not displeased when I could hear through the open door the few remarks made by the landlord and the customers at the bar.

'Well, this is leap year,' said a gruff voice.

'Yes, and more than that,' said another voice, exceedingly shrill, and evidently belonging to an old woman, 'this is the 29th of February. I wonder if *she* was in the field this evening?'

'Gammon,' said the landlord.

'Oh yes, it's all very fine for you men,' urged the shrill voice, 'you'll believe nothing but what you can eat and drink and put into your pockets; but I tell you she's sure to be in the field about nightfall, on the 29th of February.'

'Go along,' said the gruff voice. 'Why, I've been through Swampy Field over and over again, and I never seed nothing.'

'Of course not,' assented the landlord.

'Ay, ay,' pursued the shrill voice; 'but did you ever go through the field at nightfall, on the 29th of February? Were you there this evening?'

'Well, no; I can't say I was,' replied the gruff voice.

'No; exactly,' persisted the shrill old dame. 'And are you quite sure you were there at nightfall this day four year – or the day four year before that?'

'Well, I don't want to say what ain't right and straight,' replied the gruff voice, in a somewhat discomfited tone.

'And that's the wisest thing you've said yet,' replied the shrill voice, reproachfully. 'Better people than you or I have seen ghosts and been ghosts before this, to say nothing of poor Miss Crackenbridge.'

Now my moral position, as I listened to the above conversation, with my eyes fixed on the umbrella, was far from elevated. I felt at once that the 'she' of whom the old woman spoke could be no other than the mysterious female from whom I had received the gingham article that lay open before me, steaming away its moisture. I therefore knew that the sneers of the gruff gentleman and of the landlord were unjust, and yet I dared not openly enlist myself on the side of truth. My evidence was all that the old woman required to save her from derision, and I was base enough not to give it. The more I think of my conduct on that occasion, the more does my self-respect diminish. If I had been in some primitive hamlet, where the existence of ghosts is admitted as a matter of course, there is no doubt I should have come out boldly with my narrative, and should have done my best to browbeat any unlucky sceptic. My conduct,

I am convinced, would have been analogous had I been at a party of fashionable spiritualists. But here I was in a village, too closely in connection with London to admit of a primitive credulity, save among the oldest inhabitants, while the social status of the speakers was not high enough to render them pervious to aristocratic spiritualism. For fear of incurring the sneer of a vulgar landlord and his more vulgar customer, I allowed truth to be assailed without uttering a word in its defence, though I could scarcely help fancying that the umbrella was conscious of my pusillanimity, and was observing me with silent contempt.

What a great man must a martyr be, who will undergo popular execration, death, and torture, rather than keep his lips close, when they can be opened for the assertion of a truth! What an immeasurable difference there must be between my constitution and that of – say St Lawrence.[21]

But while my moral courage was at the lowest ebb, it was high water with my curiosity. Such was my utter depravity, that the circumstances that depressed the nobler quality allowed the lower one to flourish with full vigour. I sneaked out of the parlour to the bar, endeavoured to ingratiate myself by asking for something cheap that I did not want (a biscuit, I think it was), and then with the grossest affectation of vagueness, propounded the following question:

'Excuse the liberty, but did not I overhear – unintentionally, of course – something about some person who walked in some field in some remarkable manner?'

'That's right, master,' replied a man in a shaggy great-coat.

'Oh yes, quite correct,' said the landlord, 'but for further particulars you had better address yourself to this good lady here. You know there's some sort of knowledge that thrives best in the heads of elderly ladies,' he added with a wink.

I am overwhelmed with shame and confusion when I write down the humiliating fact that I actually – winked in return. If I were a member of Parliament, I wonder whether I should ever, by the remotest chance, find myself voting with the minority!

'Oh, the gentleman is quite welcome to hear the story if he likes,' said the old lady: a most respectable inoffensive-looking person. '*I* don't care for a laugh or two.'

How unworthy was I to walk on the same soil with that heroic old woman!

I shall not repeat the words of her narrative, for it was somewhat prolix, and abounded in details that did not bear directly on the main subject. It will be sufficient to state that according to the excellent lady's belief, one Miss Catherine Crackenbridge had, on the 29th of February, many years before, gone out to meet a clandestine lover, and had been seen to cross Swampy Field. Since that time, nothing had been heard of her. Some supposed that she was entrapped and murdered by a designing villain; some, that she met with a fatal accident; some, that she committed suicide. This much was certain: that every 29th of February, her figure might be seen – in fact, must be seen – to cross Swampy Field about nightfall, by any person who happened to be on the spot.

After exchanging a look of bland superiority with the landlord – despicable being that I was! – I asked if the ghost were in the habit of carrying an umbrella.

'Ho-ho-ho!' roared the landlord. 'Why, of course it would, if it went out on a wet evening like this. Well, that's a good 'un. The gentleman has given it her there, and no mistake; hasn't he, Jim?'

The man in the shaggy great-coat grunted his assent, with a low chuckle. And there was I – wretch that I was – allowing myself to be applauded for inflicting a stupid sarcasm on a defenceless female, when I firmly believed every word of her statement, and was merely endeavouring to satisfy my curiosity with reference to my strangely acquired treasure. I even joined in the laugh, and allowed them all, the old woman included, to believe that I regarded myself as an exceedingly witty and facetious person. The old woman merely observed that she knew nothing about umbrellas, and left the house in a state of irascibility that was not only justifiable, but highly laudable. As for me, I swaggered back into the parlour with the air of a conqueror by whom a worthy adversary has been valiantly demolished.

My surprise was not small when I perceived that the umbrella had changed its position during the conversation at the bar. I had left it with the convex side towards the fire, and consequently the handle in the opposite direction. Now, the handle was towards the fire, and the convex surface of gingham towards the door. As no one had entered the room, this movement was perfectly astounding, yet I did not utter a single ejaculation. I snatched up the umbrella, boldly tucked it under my arm, and stalked through the bar, bidding a hasty farewell to the landlord, and making the utterly frivolous remark that I did not think I should miss the train. If all the ghosts of all the Hamlets had stood in visible shape before me, I would rather have walked through them, than have committed myself to a word, look, or gesture, that could have compromised me in the eyes of the landlord and his gruff acquaintance. As it was, the initial letters C.C. carved on the handle, confirmed my belief that the umbrella had been the property of the ill-starred Catherine Crackenbridge.

The umbrella, I may observe – though of gingham – was of no common order. Its ivory handle was extremely massive, and richly adorned with that elaborate tracery that seems to betoken an Oriental origin. The initial letters to which I have referred had not been scratched on with the first sharp instrument that came to hand, but had been elegantly carved.

Hence it was no wonder, that when I called on my old friend Jack Slingsby, to whose residence I proceeded as soon as I quitted the train, he exclaimed, in his usual elegant style:

'Why, old boy, that's a stunning gingham you've got there. Well, it *is* an out-and-outer!'

'Yes, it is rather a good one,' I answered, with despicable indifference; and I put it in the corner near the door, and hung my hat upon it, in conformity with an old habit of mine. Being of a careless disposition, I lost many an umbrella in early youth. To prevent the recurrence of such accidents, I now adopt the expedient of using my umbrella as a hat peg, whenever I make a visit. I cannot easily forget my hat, nor can I take my hat without handling my umbrella.

'Well, but you don't mean to tell me,' pursued Jack, 'that you bought that article with your own money? A purchase of that kind is not like my old friend Yorick Zachary Yorke.'

'No; I did not purchase it – it – it came from India,' I replied, devoutly hoping, with the little conscience that was left me, that I had not told an absolute falsehood; for, indeed, it might have come from India in the first instance for anything I knew to the contrary.

The intelligence I had to communicate was of a pleasant kind, and Jack proved its exhilarating effect by ordering oysters for two, and a liberal supply of stout. When this supper, with the addition of a tumbler or so of grog, had been disposed of, I rose to depart.

'Why, old fellow,' said the hospitable Jack, 'where have you put your hat and your umbrella? Bless my soul, here they are! Well, now, I would have sworn in any witness box that you put the umbrella in the corner near the door, and then clapped your hat on the handle, and now – lo and behold! – here's the hat on the floor in the corner next the fireplace, and the umbrella, with the point inside the hat, and the handle against the wall!'

The little incident in the parlour of the Jolly Navigators had too well prepared me for such freaks on the part of my umbrella, to allow me to be taken aback. 'It is just as I put it, Jack,' I said, with heedless effrontery. 'You put a little too much brandy in your tumbler, and that, coming directly after the stout – '

Jack was fully as sober as I was, and as for the brandy and water, it had been offensively weak.

'I suppose you are right, old fellow,' interrupted Jack, with a sceptical expression of countenance. 'As the umbrella is a little damp, it was kind of you to save my carpet, by using your hat as a basin.'

Simpering out some inanity about a friend's interests being as dear to me as my own, I got out of the house as well as I could. That I had not succeeded in obliterating from Jack's mind the remembrance of the change of corners, was afterwards made evident enough. Though he never saw the umbrella again, he never met me without some question about its whereabout, or some reference to the odd occurrence of *that* evening.

I had been so much occupied hitherto in wearing a mask before other persons, that I really had not had time enough to feel all the super-natural horror that the possession of the umbrella should have inspired. Here was an article placed in my hand, by a mysterious female figure, that had vanished like a ghost, and that figure exactly corresponded to the description of a ghost current in the immediate neighbourhood! These circumstances began to impress themselves more forcibly on my mind, when, on reaching home, I found myself alone in my bachelor sitting room. The umbrella, which rested against my chair, appeared to me in the light of an unpleasant acquaintance, whom one cannot conveniently bow out, and whom one will not press to stop. What should I do with the umbrella? I did not wish to sit up with it all night, still less was I inclined to take it into my bedroom. I looked reflectively at the umbrella until I almost fancied it looked at me in return.

At last I bethought me of a little room on the floor over my bed-chamber, which was occasionally used for the deposit of lumber. Thither would I at once take my umbrella, and then redescend to the sleeping apartment. How cautiously I carried it! I felt morbidly afraid of waking the servants, who slept in the chamber adjoining the lumber room. I opened the door with a minimum of noise, that only a burglar ought to attain. I could almost fancy I was breaking into my own house.

Lumber, insignificant by day, is ghastly at night, when illuminated by a single candle, and seen by a single spectator. The common household articles, cast aside as unavailable for immediate use, and huddled together in a fashion totally at variance with their original purpose, have a corpse-like appearance, and the shadows they cast are portentous. A cobweb floating about in their vicinity is an uncomfortable phenomenon, and the lonely spectator shrinks instinctively from anything like contact with that almost intangible substance, which seems to be compounded of feathers, gossamer, and nothing, and goes by the name of 'fluff.'

I delicately placed the umbrella against a hamper, richly embroidered with cobwebs, and crept down to my bedroom: not without over-hearing the whispering voices of the servants, who had no doubt remarked the unwonted sound of footsteps.

My dreams were disagreeable enough. The umbrella seemed to stand before me as a huge many-armed bat, the gingham forming the texture of the wings, and a little claw being visible at each of the corners. Then the bat would assume the shape of a human skeleton, still many-armed, like some hideous Indian deity: with this difference, that the arms were not in a vertical circle, but were ranged around the neck, like the spokes of a horizontal wheel. And by a strange movement the nob had quitted its place, and stationed itself on the point, where it became a skull, and hattered its jaws, as if in unseemly mirth.

I was far from gratified next morning, when the servant, besides coffee and toast, brought in the umbrella, with the words, 'I think you left this in the lumber room?' I dryly answered 'Yes,' but I felt that my answer gave no satisfaction. Though the girl talked of '*leaving* the umbrella,' she must have known very well that I put it in the lumber room on purpose.

'You found the umbrella leaning against the hamper?' I asked.

'No, it was against the large trunk on the opposite side,' replied the girl.

'Of course,' I said. And never did that very common expression seem less fitted to the context of a dialogue.

An umbrella that has been lent by a ghost, which *will* be dreamed about under the most unpleasant aspect, and which, without the aid of human hands, *will* shift from one corner of a room to another, is not a desirable possession. Many were my efforts to get rid of my gingham treasure, but they were all in vain. I left it at the house of friend after friend, and frequently took away with me a silk umbrella in its stead, but it was invariably sent back. I have gone into some of the lowest streets in London, have made some trifling purchase of a marine storeseller who was obviously a receiver of stolen goods – I have placed the umbrella against his counter, and have hurried away at my quickest pace; but the light of honesty has flashed at once into the abode of roguery and crime. A ragged boy or girl has run frantically after me, with my umbrella. I have gone to umbrella makers, and have offered to sell or exchange the remarkable specimen of their art, which I carried in my hand. But never was the master of the shop at home when I called, and never had he left any person authorised to effect an exchange or a purchase. I could always find someone in charge, with full authority to sell any number of umbrellas; but I could never find anybody entrusted with power to buy one, or take one in exchange.

It struck me at last, that I would take it to the nearest pawnbroker, and offer it as a pledge for a sum too small to be refused. I had never until then visited an establishment of the sort, and I felt nervous as I approached the door – more nervous when a friend, who seemed almost to rise out of the pavement, suddenly shook me by the hand, and asked me where I was going? When I had quitted him, he stopped and looked after me, so that I was not able to dash boldly into the shop, but lingered at neighbouring windows, contemplating objects wholly devoid of interest. How long I looked at some pigs' pettitoes in one shop, and at some blacking bottles in another, I cannot conjecture. At last, assuming that I was wholly unobserved, I entered the temple of interested benevolence.

'Well, sir,' said the young man at the counter, with an air more patronising than is assumed by the generality of tradesmen towards their customers; 'what can we do for *you*?'

'I merely come to – ' thus I began, when I perceived that my umbrella was not under my arm. I rushed out of the shop leaving my sentence unfinished, and met my friend returning from his expedition. Though he merely made some commonplace remark, I could see by his manner that he had distinctly perceived my egress, and, chancing to look back towards the shop, I could see the young man's face protruding from the doorway, watching me with evident suspicion. My situation was miserable. Before me stood an old friend of the family, a warm opulent dreadfully respectable man, eyeing me with diminished respect; behind me was an utter stranger, conjecturing that I was a thief.

When I got home my umbrella was in the stand in the passage. Perhaps I had left it there. I cannot positively say whether I did or not, but something told me that it would be useless to make any other attempt to deposit it as a pledge.

As the end of another February approached, a happy thought occurred to me. Why should I not, on the anniversary of the day that had enriched me with the umbrella, take a turn in Swampy Field and restore it to the rightful owner? Though the umbrella had been placed in my hand on the 29th of February, a day that occurs only once in four years, I could regard the 1st of March as a very fair anniversary. There is this in common between the 29th of February in leap year and the 1st of March in other years – that they both follow the 28th of February. And there was no reason to suppose that a spirit, habituated to regard the essence of things, would regard a chronological arrangement merely made to adapt the calendar to mortal purposes.

I left London by railway, and on the evening of the 1st of March I was in Swampy Field with my umbrella up. There was not a cloud in the sky, and so bright was the moon that the country could be seen as by daylight. Nevertheless, I walked up and down the field with my umbrella, at full spread. No object appeared, save a group of boys, who took advantage of the bright moonlight to extend their hours of play, and who noticed me as a ridiculous figure. An umbrella held up at noon under a broiling sun, answers the purpose of a parasol, and brings no contempt on him who holds it; but a man who walks up and down a field by moonlight beneath a perfectly cloudless sky, with an outspread umbrella in his hand, is guilty of an absurdity that no one is bound to tolerate. The derision of the boys I endured with the fortitude of one who knows that he is in the wrong, and who justly merits whatever befalls him. When their verbal sallies were followed by missiles of mud and stone I retreated, without the slightest feeling of anger against my small persecutors. Had I been in their place, I should have thrown missiles also.

Months and months passed away. Every night I had dreamed of the skeleton and the bat, and the dreams had lost their terror. I believe that if I had lain from night till morning, without a visit from the familiar spectre, I should have felt my rest incomplete. As for the umbrella, I had so often put it in one corner and found it in another, that I looked at its locomotion as a matter of course; and if I had chanced to find it in the place where I had left it, my sensations would have been like those of a man whose watch has unaccountably stopped.

One evening, as my eye glanced at the advertising columns of the newspaper, it stopped at the following mysterious announcement. I beg to state, before quoting it, that on the previous day the umbrella had come back to me in a very remarkable manner. I had left it at a shop to have it newly covered with silk in the place of gingham. It had come home (as it appeared to me of its own accord), and had brought a man with it who waited in the passage to be paid the price of this alteration, and who declined to quit the premises without receiving such price. On being offered the umbrella instead, he replied, 'Blow the umbrella; I've umbrellas enough *that I can't get rid of*, I wants my money.' (From the words I have italicised, might it not almost seem as if this uncultivated person had also encountered the spectre? I merely throw out the suggestion, without insisting on it.)

'On the 29th of February, C.C. will call on Y.Z.Y., and claim the deposit.'

This was the advertisement on which my eye fell.

Now, it is not everyone that can own a property in the initials Y.Z.Y. Indeed, I am inclined to believe that I, Yorick Zachary Yorke, am their sole legitimate owner.

How great is the power of habit! Three years before, my mind had been so occupied with the extra day of the bissextile, that I had even tried to make a 29th of February of my own, by giving a new figure to the 1st of March. Now, on the contrary, I was slow in recalling to mind the connection between the umbrella and the date of its acquisition; and I believe a quarter of an hour elapsed before I recognised in C.C., the initials of the ill-starred Miss Catherine Crackenbridge.

The whole horror of four years ago was forced back upon me. My agony reached its crisis, when, looking at the date of the paper, I shrieked aloud – 'The 29th of February is today!' Frantically I rushed into the passage, took the umbrella from its stand, and placed it on the table before me. My eyes were fixed upon it so firmly that every other object faded, and my arms were not only folded, but firmly pressed together, that I might be fully aware of the strength of my own resolution.

How long I sat in this state I know not, but after a while I began to feel that I was not alone, though I could not perceive a companion. And there was a strange inconsistency in the appearance of the room. The looking glass was over the chimneypiece, and the various articles of furniture were in their places, but the carpet seemed made of wet grass, and the walls were transparent, affording a view of a flat country, in the last light of evening. I could hear the sound of rain, and could feel the drops. In defiance of all the laws of possibility, I was in two places at once – in my room in London, and on Swampy Field. A heavy weight rested on my arm, a cold breath was on my cheek, and close beside me was a pale face that moved its lips, as if speaking with the greatest earnestness; but it gave no sound.

When the face had melted away, and the weight was removed from my arm, and the carpet was free from wet grass, and the walls had ceased to be transparent, the umbrella was gone!

I am not aware whether any so-called philosophical explanation of these astonishing experiences may be attempted. I believe I have related them (on the whole) with great accuracy. If I have at all enlarged on any trifling detail, or if any deduction should be claimed by the determined sceptic, on the score of harmless stout, or of brandy and water that I have myself described as (I quote the exact words) 'offensively weak,' or on the score of a rather confused memory, or a slight habit of absence of mind, or an indigestive disposition (inherited on the father's side) to doze after dinner, there will still remain this extraordinary circumstance to be accounted for by ordinary laws – that I never could get rid of the umbrella (gingham) during the whole interval between bissextile and bissextile, and that I unaccountably and inexplicably lost the umbrella (silk) on the 29th of February, the very day when it came home from being newly covered, and brought with it the extraordinary man I have described.

HIS BLACK BAG
[by Charles Allston Collins]

I

Creel was a ducal house – a palace almost – in the north of Scotland, and I don't believe that anywhere in the north or the south, the east or the west, a pleasanter place could be found to stay at, or a pleasanter host and hostess than the Duke and Duchess of Greta. I had known the duchess long before her marriage, and as to her husband, we got on well from the very first day of my stay at Creel, when I had the good fortune to land a salmon in a style the duke highly approved of; an achievement which I followed up by tying a fly with which he himself killed first and last five large salmon, and a dozen grilse, before it came to pieces. Every year I went to stay at Creel, making one of a great society, the castle being big enough to hold a small world within its walls.

The first day of my arrival at Creel on the occasion of which I am writing, I found myself seated between old Lady Salteith, who is very deaf, and an uncommonly stupid master of foxhounds, whose voice nobody would ever care to hear unless when it was raised in a melodious tally-ho or uttering words of encouragement to a despondent hound. Exactly opposite to where I sat was the beautiful Miss Crawcour. Of this young lady I had heard a great deal, though I had never before found myself in her company. She was placed next to the man of all others for whom I have, I think, the least liking. This was Lord Sneyd, the best match, pecuniarily, and the worst, I should imagine, in every other way, that England had to show. At a glance, I saw what was going on. Miss Crawcour was a near relation of the duchess, and the duchess was one of the most inveterate matchmakers that ever lived. She was at this time about five or six-and-thirty, good-looking, and good-natured to an excess, but she had this quality of matchmaking developed in her nature to an extent that was almost inconceivable, and certainly premature.

But the duchess did not stand alone in keeping a watchful eye over this affair. My fox-hunting friend, from whom I learnt who the young lady opposite really was, had even his stupid old eye fixed upon Miss Crawcour. Lady Salteith, deaf, as I have said, and so shut out from conversation, watched her with might and main, and so, indeed, more or less, did most of the guests assembled round that great table. I ought, perhaps, to except the duke, who, I think, was insensible to all such matters, being a sportsman and nothing else in the world. The curiosity of the rest of the company was excusable. One of the special beauties of the day, and one of the great matches of the year, were there side by side, and of course everybody wanted to know what would come of it.

The beauty of Mary Crawcour was of no ordinary kind, and there was in it a wonderful sense of health and vitality. It was scarcely possible to look at her without feeling inclined to envy her the extraordinary resources and the prosperous future that an organism so complete seemed to promise. What a pity, one could not help thinking – what a pity it would be if anything should occur to mar such a career. And then as you looked from her to her neighbour the thought immediately followed, 'How mar a career more utterly than by such an alliance as that?'

Philip, Earl of Sneyd, was not what some people would call bad-looking, though to me I must own that his appearance was most disagreeable. I suppose at the time I am speaking of he was two or three-and-forty, but he was one of those light-complexioned men who look less than their age. His features, too, were small and regular. What much uglier men I have seen whom it was pleasanter to look at than this same Lord Sneyd. There was something so utterly unmanly and weak about him. He was so much too soigné[22] in his 'get up.' His hair was curled and crimped, and so were his whiskers. He affected jewellery, and I have frequently seen him with rings outside his gloves. He always wore, too, such tightly strapped trousers and such thin lacquered boots. I don't believe he had such a thing as a shooting jacket or a pair of highlows in his possession. When the other men of the party of which he made one, were out of doors, he was to be found in the drawing room playing on the piano, or, still better, getting some lady to accompany him while he sang; for I must do him the justice to say that he had a good tenor voice, and performed upon it in tune and with considerable taste.

I looked on then at this game, and I saw, or thought I saw – what? A used-up man who had never had anything but a pippin[23] for a heart – this said pippin having once, however, had some juice and softness in it, but now resembling those of Normandy, which one sees in the grocers' shops – dry, hard, and sadly contracted and pinched about the core. I saw that this man had settled with himself that the young lady beside him was personally and otherwise suitable to the position of Countess of Sneyd, and that to be the proprietor of such a piece of humanity would be generally agreeable to his inclination, and creditable to his discernment into the bargain. I saw, too, a young girl, at the very commencement of what might be a bright and glorious existence, about to sacrifice all her happiness, deliberately selling it for money and a coronet, and I thought I saw that this was not done willingly as some girls do such acts, but because she was forced into it.

Sitting there opposite, and having little to do in the way of conversation myself, I heard many scraps of dialogue between Miss Crawcour and her neighbour. The young lady was attentive to what Lord Sneyd said, certainly, but always with a grave attention. She never smiled, or relaxed.

A great dinner! What a wondrous jumble of sound, what a queer mixture of words and thoughts, of observations made aloud and observations made in secret. What scraps overheard. What nonsense. If sound and thought and action could be photographed – caught in some camera obscura, and retained, what would be the result of the process? In the case with which we have now to do – something of this sort. Quick! The instrument is set, the slide withdrawn, and the sensitive, and prepared, plate exposed.

LADY SALTEITH (to me). Did they have the same house last season? – MYSELF (bawling). No. They didn't come to town at all. – BUTLER (over right shoulder). Champagne, sir, or sparkling 'ock?[24] – MYSELF (to myself). Feverish last night; (to Butler) Neither. – LADY SALTEITH (to me). Well, they couldn't have taken a nicer house. – MYSELF (to myself). It's no use putting her right; (to Lady S., bawling louder) No. – LORD SNEYD (to Miss Crawcour). I dislike travelling. One has to rough it so. I have an aversion to roughing it. – MISS CRAWCOUR (to Lord Sneyd, coldly). But surely that is the great fun of travelling. – MYSELF (to

51

myself). Effeminate beast that Sneyd is; (to servant, silently protruding stewed pigeons over left shoulder) No, thanks. – LORD SNEYD (to Miss Crawcour). Don't see any fun in having greasy hot water instead of soup, and beds so damp that you may take a bath in them. These sort of things disturb me, put me out, make me – not angry exactly, I'm never angry – are you? – MISS CRAWCOUR. Yes, often. – LORD SNEYD. Really, now, Miss Crawcour. – BUTLER (over right shoulder). Sherry, sir? – MYSELF. Yes. – LADY SALTEITH (to neighbour on the other side). Mumbles so, everybody does, nowadays. Why can't they speak out? – LORD SNEYD (to Miss Crawcour). How does it feel being angry? – MISS CRAWCOUR. Oh, not very dreadful. I never go beyond wishing that the person I am angry with was at the other end of the world. – LORD SNEYD (calmly). Is that all? Oh, I often go as far as that myself. I should like at least half of my friends to be at the other end of the world. – MYSELF (to myself). How she hates him; (to servant, protruding curry over left shoulder) No. – GENERAL ACCOMPANIMENT. Muffled clash, respectful clatter, buzzing, and subdued laughter. – MASTER OF FOXHOUNDS (to me). Shall you be in England for the hunting season? – MYSELF. Don't intend to hunt next season. – M. F. H. What's become of that chestnut of yours? – MYSELF. Sold her. – LADY SALTEITH (to me). Miss Crawcour is not so pretty as she was last year. – MYSELF (observing Miss Crawcour to be listening). I can't agree with you there, Lady Salteith; (to myself) I've never seen her before, by the by; (to servant, protruding mutton over left shoulder) Yes. – BUTLER (over right shoulder). Champagne or sparkling 'ock, sir? – MYSELF. Neither. – LORD SNEYD (to Miss Crawcour). Did you hear Lady Salteith just now (his lordship was devouring curry when Lady Salteith spoke and is only now ready to talk)? – MISS CRAWCOUR. Yes. – LORD SNEYD. Does *that* make you angry? – MISS CRAWCOUR. No. Lady Salteith is quite right. – GENERAL ACCOMPANIMENT. Muffled clash, respectful clatter, and subdued laughter. – M. F. H. I know a man who would have given you anything for that chestnut. – MYSELF. Yes? Well, it's too late now. I sold him very well. – BUTLER (over right shoulder). Sherry, sir? – MYSELF. Thanks. – LADY SALTEITH (to me). Not a good complexion, has she? – MYSELF (shouting). I can't agree with you, Lady Salteith. – LADY SALTEITH. Yes, as you say, wants colour. MYSELF (to myself). It's no use; (to servant, protruding grouse over left shoulder) If you please. – LORD SNEYD (to Miss Crawcour). What are you going to do tomorrow morning, Miss Crawcour? Will you try that air from the Prophète[25] with me again? – MISS CRAWCOUR. In the morning I am going out riding, Lord Sneyd. – LORD SNEYD. Dear me. You are always riding. I hate riding, it shakes one so. Well, in the afternoon, then, after luncheon? – MISS CRAWCOUR (icily). After luncheon I shall be quite ready. – MYSELF (to myself, being inclined for meditation). That girl speaks with the air of a martyr. If I had been Lord Sneyd – (to servant, protruding Charlotte-Russe[26] over left shoulder) No – (to myself) I would have made an effort to accompany myself in that air from the Prophète, or have sought a more willing coadjutor; (to servant, protruding jelly over left shoulder) No, thank you. – GENERAL ACCOMPANIMENT. Muffled clash, respectful clatter, buzzing, and subdued laughter. – M. F. H. (to a neighbour). We've begun the cub hunting now regularly. My huntsman tells me there are a good many foxes this year. – NEIGHBOUR (another fox-hunter, indistinctly reported by the instrument). Glad – hear it – good f. country – plenty – cover. – LADY SALTEITH (to me). Do you ever see my nephew now? – MYSELF. What, Harry Rushout? Oh yes, sometimes. – LADY SALTEITH (to her neighbour on the other side). My nephew is the wildest young man about town. The other day he got brought up before the magistrate and – LORD SNEYD (to Miss Crawcour). Lady Salteith is not always so fortunate as she might be in the subjects she chooses for conversation. – MISS CRAWCOUR. Poor thing. She belongs to a different time. But she's very good, really. – LORD SNEYD. I wonder she comes out, so deaf as she is. She ought to stop at home. – MISS CRAWCOUR. I like Lady Salteith exceedingly, and am always glad to be staying in the house with her. – MYSELF. That's right. – GENERAL ACCOMPANIMENT. Clash – clatter.

Enough! Down goes the slide. The instrument is shut up. There is the result of the operation.

When that long 'banquet scene' was at an end, and the ladies left the room, I found myself, by the retirement of old Lady Salteith, next my hearty straightforward manly friend Jack Fortescue, with whom I had already exchanged a nod behind the old lady's back. I was very glad to see him. We talked about all sorts of things, and presently got upon the subject that had been occupying me so much during dinner. I was rather anxious, I must own, to lead to it, having heard a rumour somewhere or other, that my friend Jack himself was smitten with Miss Crawcour. I don't know when I had heard it, or where. Those things seem in some societies to circulate in the air.

To my surprise, I found Fortescue very uncommunicative about this matter, and still more, to my wonder, I observed a tendency in him rather favourable to this match. He even sought to defend Lord Sneyd against my attacks.

'Oh, he's not such a bad fellow,' he said, 'when you come to know him. He's affected, you know, and pretends to be wonderfully refined, and to be a petit-maître,[27] and all that, but he has his good points. We fellows who are always shooting, or fishing, or riding over stone dykes, are apt to undervalue a man of quieter tastes, and more sedentary pursuits. Sneyd goes in, you know, for being a sort of artist. By the by – talking of artists – did you see that portrait of the duchess in the Academy this year – wasn't it good?'

I saw that my friend wanted to get away from the subject, so of course I did not attempt to pursue it. I was not enlightened by anything that occurred in the drawing room after dinner. Miss Crawcour and Fortescue hardly exchanged a dozen words, and Lord Sneyd was in attendance upon the young lady throughout the evening. In the smoking room afterwards, Lord Sneyd refused cigars, and smoked some infernal perfumed composition out of a hookah. Heaven knows what it was. Opium, perhaps? Nothing wholesome, I'll warrant.

II

It was on the day succeeding that of my arrival at Creel, that I sought the billiard room, the usual refuge of the unemployed. I had remained at home that morning, having some letters to write and other things to do in my own room. These finished, I had still half an hour or more on my hands before luncheon, so I thought I would wend my way to the billiard room. If I found anyone to play with, so much the better. If not, I would practise difficult cannons for half an hour or so, and in that way get through the time.

Two people were in the room. A gentleman and a lady. Jack Fortescue and Miss Crawcour. They were standing together at the further end of the table. Both had cues in their hands, and the balls were on the board, but at the moment of my entrance they were certainly not playing. Miss Crawcour's back was to the light, but a glance showed me beyond a shadow of doubt that she had been crying – was crying, even, when I entered the room.

What was I to do? Fortescue was my friend. The room was public to everybody in the castle. If I retired, it would be a marked act, showing that I felt I had interrupted some scene that did not require witnesses.

'Are you having a game, or only practising?' I said to Fortescue, merely to break the awkward silence.

'Oh, it's a game,' he answered, making a great effort, but not speaking then in his proper voice. 'And it's my stroke. Look,' he said to me quickly, 'is that cannon possible?' and he made it almost as he spoke. Two or three more followed. Then a hazard. At last a bad shot, and it was time for Miss Crawcour.

She came to her place at the table, and made a violent effort to collect herself. I did not look at her, but pretended to be absorbed in marking Fortescue's score. I heard her cue strike the ball in an uncertain way. There was no subsequent sound indicating the contact of her ball with one of the others. It was a miss. The moment she had made it, she placed her cue against the wall, and saying something indistinctly about not being able to play, and about my finishing the game instead of her, left the billiard room, closing the door after her.

As soon as she was gone, Fortescue came up to where I stood.

'After what you've seen,' he said, 'it's no use my attempting to make a secret of what has been going on between Miss Crawcour and myself.'

'My dear Fortescue, I have no wish to force myself on your confidence. What I have seen, can be forever as if I had not seen it, if you wish it. You know that.'

'No, no, I don't wish it,' he answered quickly. 'But come outside with me for half a minute. We can't talk here.'

Out in the open air, the rooks cawing about the treetops as their nests waved to and fro in the wind, he spoke again, as we lay on the grass.

'I dare say you have heard my name and Miss Crawcour's spoken of together? – You have. I don't know what right anyone has had to talk about either of us. However, that can't be helped.' He paused, and did not seem able to go on.

'I hate speaking of things of this sort,' he continued, after a moment, and in an impatient tone, 'one's words sound like words in a valentine or a trashy novel. Well – it can't be helped. I love this girl, Mary Crawcour. I would do anything for her.'

'And yet you could speak yesterday about her marrying that man Sneyd.'

'You were not then in my confidence. To the world I must seem to favour that marriage. I am pledged to do so.'

'Pledged? To whom?'

'To the duchess.'

'My dear Fortescue, how, in Heaven's name, could you enter into so rash an engagement?'

'How? How could I do otherwise, you mean? You know my position. I have two hundred a year and my pay. Can I marry that girl, accustomed to the life she *is* accustomed to, on that? Have I a right to fetter her with a long engagement, on the remote possibility of my becoming possessed of property between which and myself there are half a dozen lives? Have I a right to stand in the way of such a marriage as that with Sneyd? What could I say when the duchess put these questions to me?'

'Do you believe that Miss Crawcour would be happy in such a marriage?'

'I don't know,' answered Fortescue, almost desperately. 'I have seen such misery come from poverty in married life.'

'Depend on it,' I answered, 'it is not the worst evil, by many, many degrees. Fortescue,' I continued, after a moment's pause, 'does Miss Crawcour love you?'

'I think so,' he said, speaking in a low voice.

'Then depend on it you are doing wrong. You are acting as you think rightly, and with a great and noble self-denial. But you are mistaken, cruelly, terribly mistaken, if you have pledged yourself to favour this match with Sneyd and to give up your own hold on that young lady's love.'

'I am pledged,' Fortescue answered.

'To what?'

'To do nothing that is calculated to hinder the marriage with Sneyd, and not to press my own suit by word or deed for a period of five years – by which time, of course, all chance will be over.'

'And this was what you were telling Miss Crawcour just now?'

'Something of it. She followed me to the billiard room. She seems desperate, reckless. She swears she will not have him. I entreated her to leave me – you saw the rest.'

I said, after a moment's pause, 'The conduct of the duchess surprises me in this thing, I own. She has such good points, I know. She is kind-hearted – hospitable – '

'Yes, she is all that,' said Fortescue, interrupting me, 'but she is touched by the world like everybody else. Why, you don't know what the notions of these people are. The things that are necessaries of life to them – real necessaries of life – require a fortune to provide them. To a woman like the duchess, the existence which such means as mine imply, seems what the workhouse or absolute starvation appears to you. When the duchess puts the case so to me, I tell you, I am speechless.'

'Fortescue,' I said, after a long silence. 'These things being so, and this most rash and miserable pledge being given – what do you do here?'

'I go tomorrow.'

'Have you told Miss Crawcour that?'

'No, I have told no one. I mean to tell no one. When the party goes out riding tomorrow morning, I shall excuse myself, and – and leave this place, most likely forever. There is a row in India I hear – perhaps I shall get rid of my life there. It's at anybody's service.'

Again there was a pause. I knew what that careless tone meant, and for a time I could not speak.

'Fortescue,' I said at last, 'I have one more thing to ask. Has Sneyd spoken yet?'

'No,' answered my friend, rising to lead the way to the house; 'but he is certain to do so today – or tomorrow.'

III

That afternoon, a party, of which Fortescue and I formed two, went out cover-shooting in the neighbourhood. I never saw my friend shoot so ill. Indeed, the poor fellow seemed entirely bewildered, and unfit for anything. I think he only joined the party to get away from the house.

Miss Crawcour did not appear at dinner. She was suffering from a headache, the duchess said, and preferred remaining in her room. Lord Sneyd professed as much interest as would comport with his languid manner. I could see in Fortescue's face, carefully as he had drilled it, how much he suffered additionally at not spending this, his last evening, in Miss Crawcour's society.

The next day came, and I was again prevented, by certain literary labours to which I was obliged to devote myself, from going out in the early part of the day. I spent the morning in my room, which was situated in one of the round towers that flanked the entrance of the castle, one on each side.

About half-past eleven I heard the voices of some of the men who were staying in the castle, as they lounged about the door, gossiping and talking. Soon after, I heard the clatter of horses' hoofs in the distance, and soon the same sound accompanied by the scattering of gravel, and the 'Wo, mare!' and 'Steady horse!' of the grooms.

I looked out from behind my curtains; I am always very easily diverted from my work. The riding party was all assembled. Three of four men; among them, for a wonder, Lord Sneyd. He had his own horse, a nasty long-tailed white brute, that cost, I dare say, a mint of money, and that no man worth twopence would get across. The duchess and Miss Crawcour were the ladies of the party. The duke came to the door to see them off. He was not going with them, having all sorts of things to arrange with that important minister the gamekeeper.

'Where's Fortescue?' said someone.

'Oh, he's not going this morning,' the duke answered. 'He is writing letters.' He was helping Miss Crawcour into the saddle as he spoke. It may have been the exertion of mounting, or it may not, but I could see that she blushed deeply.

I did not like the look of the animal on which Miss Crawcour was mounted. As far as beauty went, certainly there was nothing to complain of. A handsomer mare I never saw. But the movements of the ears were too incessant and violent, and there was more white to the eye shown that I like to see in connection with a riding habit. The mare had been difficult to hold while Miss Crawcour was being lifted on, and, now that the young lady was fairly on the brute's back, it became exceedingly restive, almost unmanageable.

'Are you afraid of her at all, Mary?' the duke asked, as he stood by the door; 'she seems unusually frisky this morning.'

'No, not in the least. She's always like this at starting.'

This was Miss Crawcour's answer, but I thought she looked pale. Perhaps it was the reaction after that blush I had noticed. The duke spoke again. This time to the head groom:

'Has that mare been exercised this morning, Roberts?'

The man hesitated just half a moment, and looked at the mare.

'Yes, your grace,' he said, touching his hat.

'You're sure, Mary,' the duchess said, 'that you're not afraid? Do let them take her back and bring you another mount.'

'Yes, yes, much better,' added the duke. 'Roberts, send that mare back, and saddle Robin Hood for Miss Crawcour.'

'Beg your pardon, your grace, but the horse is in physic; he's not been very well for a day or two.'

'Well, then, the brown mare, or Bullfinch, or – '

'No, no, no, no,' Miss Crawcour called from the saddle. 'I like this mare best of all. Let her go,' she said to the groom who was holding the cursed brute's head. And off she cantered, the mare plunging and kicking.

'Really,' said Lord Sneyd, with his foot in the stirrup, 'Miss Crawcour ought not to be allowed to ride that ferocious animal. Can nobody stop her?'

'You ride after her, Sneyd,' said the duke, smiling, 'and try if you can't bring her back.' Lord Sneyd was in the saddle by this time, and cantered off at a regular rocking-horse pace, his groom behind him on a thoroughbred.

That was the last I saw of the cavalcade. The duke retired immediately to the gun room; and I went back to my writing table, but I could not help feeling a certain sense of uneasiness, the look of that mare not being at all to my liking, and the manner of the groom having left an impression on my mind that the animal had not really been out before, that morning.

All the events of that day are very fresh in my memory. The next room to mine was a boudoir. There was a piano in it, and someone of the ladies of the party was playing on it. I don't know what she was playing, though I should recognise the air now in a moment if I heard it. It was what is called a 'piece,' and had a wonderful plaintive beauty about it. As the performer played it many times over, I suppose she was learning it.

I went on writing, and what I wrote seemed in a sort of way to be mixed up with this tune. Presently I heard the sound of wheels, and some light vehicle drove up to the door. I went again to the window. It was a dog cart, driven by one of the duke's grooms, and it drew up before the door. Some servants brought out a portmanteau, some gun-cases, and other luggage, and placed them in the vehicle. Almost at the same moment my door opened, and Fortescue entered the room. I never saw anything more dreadful than the suppressed agony in his face.

'Goodbye, old fellow,' he said, with a miserable ghastly smile. 'I'm off, you see. Will you take charge of this note for the duchess? I've explained to Greta that I find my letters this morning require my presence in London. Goodbye! I've only just time to catch the train.'

'Stay,' I said; 'where can I write to you?'

'London, tomorrow. After that, Chatham. Goodbye again, dear old fellow, goodbye!'

He was gone. In a minute more I saw the duke come with him to the door, and after shaking him warmly by the hand and pressing him to return whenever he possibly could, they parted, and the dog cart disappeared rapidly, behind that angle of the castle round which I had seen Miss Crawcour pass so short a time before.

Poor fellow! what a departure. What an episode in the gay story of the life at Creel.

I went back to my desk. And still from the next room came that same plaintive air, and still it seemed to belong to what I wrote, and to be an inseparable part of the day and its events.

Once more I was disturbed, and by the clatter of hoofs. It was a single horse this time, and going evidently at a tremendous pace. I looked out and saw young Balham, who had been one of the party of equestrians, dashing along the road at full gallop. He turned off in the direction of the stables, and I saw no more of him. I remained where I was, but with a dim foreboding that something had gone wrong, and by and by a low open carriage, empty, was driven out of the stable yard at a great pace. Lord Balham rode rapidly on in front of it, both he and the carriage going back by the way he had come.

I still kept where I was, and in a few moments the door of the house was opened, and some of the servants came out. They looked out in the direction by which the carriage had disappeared. One or two ladies' maids stood on the steps, one of them the duchess's, and there was another who was crying, but quite quietly, the servants in such houses being drilled into the greatest undemonstrativeness. I heard one of the menservants say to another, 'Roberts is gone off to Inverkeed, for Dr MacIntyre, and James has gone into Creel for Mr Cameron. They'll both be here quickly.'

'Is his grace in the house?'

'No. He's up at the plantations. But he's been sent for.'

The conversation among the men stopped suddenly. The carriage, driving now very slowly, had come in sight. It was followed by some horsemen. Presently I made out that two grooms behind were leading each a lady's horse; then I saw that the duchess was sitting in the carriage bending over and supporting *something* – somebody – lying at length on the cushions. A gentleman, one of those on horseback, detached himself from the group, and rode swiftly up to the door.

'Is Miss Crawcour's maid here?' he asked.

The girl came forward, sobbing. The duchess's woman, older, with more head, more self-controlled, and more useful now, came out too.

Not a word more was spoken. The carriage drew up to the door, and I saw at a glance that it was Miss Crawcour over whom the duchess was bending; that the poor girl's habit was all torn and dirty; and that a handkerchief, deeply stained, was laid over her face.

There was no word spoken still. The duchess, in tears, descended from the carriage and went into the house to see that all was ready, while the gentlemen of the party lifted the poor maimed form of Miss Crawcour from the cushions. I noticed that Lord Sneyd did not assist in this, but hovered about the group in a helpless way. Nobody seemed to want him, or to notice him.

I remained still where I was. I knew I could be of no use, should only be in the way below. I could not help looking. I wish I had not. As they lifted Miss Crawcour from the carriage, the handkerchief that was over her face became displaced, and I saw –

One whole side of her face seemed to have been crushed and beaten in. That beautiful face!

It was covered again, in a moment, but I had seen it – and so had someone else. When Lord Sneyd looked upon that mutilated face, he turned even paler than he had been before, and went into the house.

The door closed over the sad group, with Mary Crawcour's helpless figure carried in the midst of it, the carriage drove away to the stables, and all was quiet again.

'And *he* did it, think of that,' said Balham. 'It was that disgusting white brute of his to whom this terrible mishap is owing.'

'What do you mean?' I asked, as we were talking some time afterwards about what has been partly described above. 'How did the thing happen? You saw it all.'

'It is told in two words,' said Balham. 'You know that mare that poor Miss Crawcour used to ride. Well, she was always an unsafe, ill-conditioned mare, in my opinion, but on this occasion she was particularly bad. All the time we were out she was fidgeting and starting at everything, and more than one of us wanted Miss Crawcour to let the groom put her saddle on one of the other horses, and let some man with a stronger hand ride the mare. However, it was no use, and so at last – I never saw a worse thing – the mare took fright at some barrow, or something by the side of the hedge, and bolted straight across the road at a bound. Miss Crawcour was thrown, but fell clean, luckily without becoming entangled with the stirrup, and might have escaped serious mischief, when up comes that intolerable ass Sneyd, on his infernal ambling Astley's-looking beast,[28] and rides clean over her, the brute of a horse – ssh – I can't bear to think of it – sending one of his hoofs straight into her face as he passed.'

'And her arm is broken, too, is it not?'

'Yes, I believe so. That may, however, have happened when she fell; but the other thing, that fearful mutilation of the poor young lady's face, was done by a kick from that horse of Sneyd's, and by nothing else in the world. I saw it with my own eyes.'

HIS WRITING DESK
[by Charles Allston Collins]

Some years after these things had happened, I stood on the summit of one of those mighty mountains that form a boundary line, such as few countries can boast of, between Switzerland and Italy.

It was evening, and I was gazing with all my eyes into that strange receptacle for the dead, which the monks of St Bernard have placed at the door of their convent, and where the bodies of those unfortunates who have perished in the snow are preserved. They are embalmed by the highly rarefied air of that height, and do not decay. The Egyptian mummies are not more perfectly kept.

I was so absorbed in these strange figures, that I scarcely noticed there was anyone standing beside me, until I suddenly heard my own name pronounced by a voice familiar to me. I turned and found myself face to face with Jack Fortescue.

'Well,' he said, almost before we had exchanged greetings, 'this *is* the most extraordinary thing, the most marvellous combination of coincidences, that ever took place since the creation of the world! Who do you think is in there?' pointing to the convent.

'Who,' I asked. 'In Heaven's name, who?'

'In the strangers' parlour, there, you will find, at this moment, your old acquaintance Lord Sneyd – and, what is more, a new acquaintance, if you choose to make it, in the shape of that nobleman's illustrious consort.'

'What, the Irish-Italian singer, who, as I saw by Galignani, had managed to become Lady Sneyd?'

'The same.'

'And your wife – where is she?'

'Mary is with me. Is it not extraordinary, incredible almost, that we should all be under the same roof again? Do you remember the last time?

'Of course,' Fortescue went on, 'I can't let her come in contact with those people, so she keeps her room, or rather her cell. It is awfully cold, but anything is better than such a meeting.'

'But you will let me see her?'

'*You.* Why, of course,' Fortescue answered. 'How can you ask?'

'I will ask something else, then,' I continued. 'I will ask you to tell me some of the particulars of what took place after I left Creel, and went abroad. My letters from England and the papers told me, to my great delight, of your marriage with Miss Crawcour, and also of Lord Sneyd's wonderful match. But I want to know more than these bare facts.'

'There really is not much to tell,' said Fortescue. 'When I got your letter telling me of that terrible disaster at Creel, I was at Chatham, and was, in fact, just negotiating for an exchange into a regiment that was going abroad at once. Your letter altered all my plans. Do what I would, the thought of that poor maimed figure haunted me, the love that I resisted when she was in the full pride and glory of her beauty, became now that pity was mixed up with it, now that this fearful trouble had come upon her, a thing that I could no longer hold out against. I felt that I *must* go back to Creel. And I went.

'When I got there, I found that that infernal brute and scoundrel, Sneyd, had left the place. Very soon after the accident – you know that he had never actually spoken to the duke about Mary, or said anything definite to her – well, very soon after the accident, he discovered that it was actually necessary that he should pay a visit to some estates of his in Ireland. He left the castle, to come back there no more. He went first of all to Ireland, and then was absent on the Continent for a considerable length of time. There was an end of him. At Naples, he became entangled in the snares of a regular designing adventuress, and out of those snares he has never escaped. I wish him joy.

'Well, I stayed on and on at Creel. It was a quiet delightful time. After the accident everybody left, but Greta – he and I, you know, were always great friends – the duke pressed me to stay that he might have somebody to shoot with, and I stayed on, and on.

'At that time, too, I saw more of the duchess than I had ever done before, and one day we began talking about the accident and about Sneyd's behaviour, and I ventured to say that I thought that if Mary had broken every bone in her skin, she would still have reason to congratulate herself on being thereby delivered from a marriage with the wretched creature that he had proved himself to be. The duchess did not differ from me, and somehow from that day a strange kind of hope and happiness seemed to take possession of me, a curious indefinite delight such as I had never felt before.

'At length a day came when I was allowed to see *her*. And when I went into the room' – at this point Fortescue's voice faltered a little – 'when I saw her poor arm bound up, and half her sweet face covered with bandages – I knelt down by the side of the sofa, and, in short, I made a fool of myself. The duchess was present, but she was fairly beat, and – Well, very soon I was discussing ways and means with the duke.

'There never was anything like that man's kindness. Besides making Mary a very handsome present indeed, which he declared he had always intended to do, he set himself to work to get me such an appointment as should make it possible for me to marry. Between him and the duchess (whose interest is not small) this has been effected, so I waited till I got my company – I am Captain Fortescue now, if you please – and then sold my commission, and with my own small means, and my place in the Shot and Shell Department, we manage to get on in a very inexplicable but delightful way.'

'And the privations that were to make your wife so wretched?' I asked, as I shook him warmly by the hand.

'Looked much worse at a distance than they do close,' said my friend. 'I do think, sincerely,' he continued, 'that an imprudent marriage *ought* to be made every now and then, if it is only to bring out the immense amount of real kindness that there is in the world. I am perfectly sure that if two married people, however poor they may be, will only put a good face upon it, and neither sink down into gloomy despair on the one hand, nor shut themselves up in a haughty reserve on the other – I am perfectly sure, I say, that there is so much real goodness in the world, that they need never know that they are poorer than other people, or suffer any of those humiliations, the dread of which has kept many true and loving hearts asunder. But come,' said Fortescue, 'I am getting poetical. Let us go inside, and see how Lord and Lady Sneyd are getting on. He'll take no notice of either of us, you'll see.'

Fortescue left me for a time to go and see after his wife, and I went up into the strangers' room. There was a good large company assembled, waiting for the supper hour, English tourists, German students, and some French officers – among them, sure enough, sitting next to a very showy and over-dressed lady with jewellery all over her, with a very strong soupçon of paint upon her countenance, with a long curl brought over her left shoulder – there was Lord Sneyd.

A changed man already. Feeble and effeminate he was still, but he had ceased to be the insolent languid petit-maître and coxcomb he was when I had last seen him. He was lowered in tone. His whole faculties seemed to be entirely absorbed in attention on his better half, off whom he never took his eyes.

'I hear,' said Fortescue to me, as he took his place by my side at the supper table, 'that he is intensely jealous of her, and leads, in consequence, the most miserable life imaginable. Look how he is watching, now that that French officer is speaking to her. The man is only offering her some potatoes, but Sneyd looks as if he would like – if he had courage enough – to put his knife into him.'

It was true. A more pitiable and contemptible sight I never witnessed than this man's jealousy. It extended itself to the French officers opposite, to the young English undergraduate who sat next to the lady, and even to the good-looking young monk who – a perfect man of the world, and a very agreeable fellow – took the head of the supper table. I must say that Lady Sneyd's appearance was not calculated to quiet her lord and master's discomfort. A more liberal use of a pair of fine rolling black eyes I never saw made. Not long after supper this worthy pair retired, not the slightest attempt at recognition of either Fortescue or myself being made on the part of this distinguished nobleman. Perhaps he was of opinion that our fascinations would be dangerous with his amiable consort. Perhaps he felt a little ashamed of himself.

As soon as those two were gone, or at least after a reasonable interval, Fortescue addressed himself to the young monk who played the part of host, and remarked that he would go upstairs, and, if his wife were somewhat recovered from her fatigues, would persuade her to come down and get thoroughly warmed at the fire before retiring for the night.

Our host, with that interest in other people's affairs that foreigners either feel to so delightful an extent, or assume so admirably, expressed his earnest hope that 'Madame would be able to descend,' and Fortescue left the apartment.

I own that at this moment I felt somewhat nervous.

In a short time the door opened, and Fortescue appeared with his wife on his arm. She came up to me at once, and we shook hands cordially, while I spoke such words of congratulation as I had ready, which were, in truth, not very many. At one glance I saw that at all events the *expression* of her face was safe. A great matter that, at any rate.

The injury that she had sustained being from a kick, and not from a fall or dragging along on the ground, was confined entirely to one portion (the left side) of her face. That that injury had been a terrible one it was impossible not to see even now. The brow immediately over the eye was scarred, and the eyebrow something interrupted in its even sweep; the cheek was scarred and indented, and there was a slight scar on the nostril, all on this same left side; but the eye, sheltered in its somewhat sunken recess, had escaped; the mouth was unhurt, and, above all, there was the expression, the general look, of which the attractiveness had been so great. That fearful injury that I had looked down on from the turret window at Creel had left much less damage behind than one could even have hoped.

We talked pleasantly, all three together – the rest of the company having retired, and our host too – for nearly an hour. We talked of our travels, of the places to which they were bound and from which I was returning, and of a hundred other things, until the hour admonished us that it was time to part for the night.

As we rose to say 'Goodnight' – my friend and his wife standing up together – I thought I had never seen a happier or a better matched couple. Suddenly a thought seemed to strike her. She touched her wounded cheek slightly with her hand.

'Would you have known me?' she asked, smiling.

'No one can tell,' said Fortescue, interrupting my ready answer, ' how I love that precious scar' – he leaned down and touched it with his lips. 'But for that, we might not be together now. But for that, your life, Mary, might have been one of misery unutterable, and mine – if not sacrificed on the plains of India – might have been as utter a blank as that of any one of those unknown men who have entertained us here tonight.'

HIS DRESSING CASE
[by Arthur Locker]

The passengers on board the good ship *Golden Dream*, homeward bound from Melbourne, were beginning to get rather weary and tired of their trip. We were only in the fourth week of the voyage; but the month was July, the days were short, gloomy, and stormy; and the sea was covered with those mountainous waves that are to be seen in perfection off Cape Horn. The stout ship went struggling along within six points of a fierce north-easterly gale, quivering like a living creature, as the remorseless waves struck her blow after blow. On the log being hove,[29] we found that we were making barely two knots an hour; and to add to our perplexity, a sudden chill in the air, and a peculiar white glare in the horizon, informed us that we were surrounded with icebergs. Before nightfall the violence of the gale had somewhat abated, and the passengers hurried on deck to look at the first iceberg, which was within half a mile of us. It was a sight worth seeing. We beheld an enormous mass of rock-like ice, with a perpendicular wall facing us, fully three hundred feet high, against the steep sides of which the waves dashed incessantly. The colour of the iceberg was a brilliant pellucid white, except in the deep fissures and interstices where the hue was changed to cobalt, or on the summits of the precipices, which glowed in the rays of the setting sun with all the prismatic tints of the rainbow.

'Eh! man!' exclaimed an enthusiastic Scotchman. ''Tis joost Edinburgh Castle to the life!'

'What a fortune a fellow could make among the Melbourne confectioners, if he could only tow it into Port Phillip during the hot weather,' remarked a prosaic colonist.

'Well, it's a pretty sight,' said an old lady, 'a very pretty sight! But I wish they'd all sink to the bottom at night, and come up again in the morning.'

'It would be very convenient indeed, ma'am,' answered the third mate. 'It would save our eyes tonight considerably, for we shall have to keep a bright lookout.'

We passed a very gloomy evening. The wind had almost fallen to a calm, while the sea continued to run extremely high, causing the ship to roll terribly. Everything that was not securely fixed was flying about the cabin, the destruction of crockery was appalling, and the steward passed the interval between supper and bedtime in a state of despair, chasing cups, saucers, and bottles. Even the four passengers who clung to whist every evening with a devotion befitting the renowned Sarah Battle[30] were forced to give up their game. Even chess, though played on a board provided with spring fastenings, was found impracticable. The chessboard sprang up bodily, pieces and all, made a somersault in the air, darted into the cabin of a married couple who were putting their baby to bed, extinguished their candle-lamp, and frightened their cockatoo into hysterics.

For myself, I went on deck, and there, sheltered by the penthouse that overhung the main deck at the extremity of the poop,[31] endeavoured to solace myself with a pipe. I was very glad to hear a voice out of the pitchy darkness saying,

'Nasty thick night, sir.'

It was Tom White, an able seaman, and one of the greatest growlers on board.

'What do you think of the weather, Tom?' I asked him.

''Bout as bad as it can be. If it had kept on to blow, it might have took us through all this here ice; but now it's fallen calm, the bergs will gather round the ship, just as the bits of stick in a pond get round a dead cat. Ah! Once let me set foot ashore, and you'll never catch me round the Horn again.'

Poor Tom! I dare say he had uttered this declaration five hundred times before, and had always forgotten it when signing articles at the shipping office.

'I hope they're keeping a bright lookout forward, Tom?'

'A bright lookout! How can they? Why, the night's as thick as a tub of Dutch butter. Then it ain't these big lumps as I'm afeard of. If the lookouts ain't asleep, or yarning, they might chance to see *them*. What I funk,[32] is the nasty little sneaking bits of ground-ice, about the size of a ship's long-boat.'

'Surely they would not injure a stout ship like this, Tom?'

'Stout ship? Ha, ha! Why, this is a softwood ship – a regular New Brunswicker.[33] She'd have no more chance again the ice, than a chaney cup again a soup-and-bully tin;[34] and then, with all this here copper ore in her inside, down she'd go – and you along with her.'

'And you too, Tom.'

'Well, I don't know about that. Sailors ain't like passengers. There's the boats to cut adrift. Besides, I'm on deck, and you'd be below, smothered like a rat in his hole.'

With a series of parting growls Tom White disappeared in the darkness, leaving me in a very uncomfortable frame of mind. I was half inclined at first to stay on deck all night, but eventually determined to go below, and seek oblivion from danger in sleep.

I envied my cabin companion, the fat German, Schlafenwohl. He lay in profound slumber, while his nose trumpeted defiance to the creaking of the timbers and the dashing of the waves. Taking advantage of a favourable lurch, I clambered up to my berth, which was over the German's head. I tried to think of everything I could recall to my memory, unconnected with ship life, but the horrible snoring of my companion and the lurches of the ship destroyed all prospect of repose. I repeated verses from the most soporific poets I could remember. I counted numbers, and got up as far as six hundred and fifty-four, when suddenly the ship rolled more frightfully than she had done yet. I felt that she was heeling completely over, and that the mainyard[35] must be dipping in the waves. A fearful crashing of plates and dishes was succeeded by the still more terrible sound of rushing water. I opened my eyes, which I had until now kept obstinately closed. To my horror I discovered that the porthole, instead of being at my side, was directly above my head. I unscrewed the port and thrust my head out. I was appalled by what I beheld. The ship was on her beam-ends, and her masts were disappearing beneath the angry sea. There was no time to be lost. Fortunately I had turned in in my day clothes, boots excepted, so I climbed through the porthole, which barely permitted the passage of my body, and lay clinging to the wet slippery side of the vessel. A thought struck me. Shall I waken Schlafenwohl? No; I might lose my own life in endeavouring to save his. His ample figure could never pass the narrow porthole. It is astonishing how selfish men are apt to become at such times. I murmured, '*Requiescat in pace*,'[36] and gazed around me once more.

71

The vessel was sinking rapidly. Her masts were now entirely under water, and only a few feet of her weather yardarm were visible. I heard a horrible grinding noise. Peering through the darkness, I beheld an immense iceberg crashing against the ship's side. I summoned all my energies, took a tremendous leap, and fell into a small cavity filled with freshly fallen snow. As soon as I recovered my feet I looked once more around. The *Golden Dream* had disappeared, and nothing was visible save a few dark objects floating on the surface of the water.

I determined to secure one of these objects. 'Possibly,' I thought, 'the harness-casks on the deck have broken adrift. They are filled with beef and pork, and the contents of one of them would support life for months.' I descended cautiously through the thick darkness, to a ledge that abutted directly on the water. The spray of the breakers was dashing in my face, and I trembled lest the frail piece of ice on which I stood, should give way beneath my feet and precipitate me into the briny abyss. I stretched out my hand – it was instantly grasped by another hand! I drew back in horror, and the force of my retrograde movement was such that I pulled the person who had clutched my hand completely out of the water.

As soon as I had deposited the unknown individual in a place of comparative safety, I demanded his name. The figure drew a long breath, and replied, 'Julius Schlafenwohl.'

I staggered back in astonishment, and exclaimed, 'Why, good Heaven, how came you here?'

'Very easily, my friend. You see I am a good diver and schvimmer, and I took my time about it.'

'Why, you've got a long rope tied round your body!'

'Pull hart upon it, and see vat you will bring op.'

I hauled as he bade me, and presently landed on the iceberg, a large case.

'You see,' continued the German, 'I am never in a hurry. Ven de sheep turned over, I turned out of my bairt myself, and den I tink to myself, Julius, you vill vant etwas essn, so I filled dis box with prog,[37] and schvam qvietly up the cabin stairs.'

'My dear Schlafenwohl!' I exclaimed, embracing him, 'how delighted I am to have been the means of saving your life!'

'Vell, I don't know about dat,' responded the stolid German, dryly; 'I could have saved myself. You see, my friend, the prog is just enough for vun – no more.'

'My noble fellow!' I replied, 'do not harbour such selfish thoughts. Remember, we are brothers in adversity, and should help each other.'

'Vot can *you* help *me* to?' asked Schlafenwohl, with a touch of sarcasm.

I stammered, 'I – I've nothing, but – yes! I have a pound of tobacco! I bought it of the steward today, and here it is, safe in the pocket where I put it.'

'Ju – vivallera!' shouted the German, enthusiastically, 'dat is just vot I have not got. Yes, my friend, we will swear brothership, and share our goods together.'

'Agreed,' I replied.

Schlafenwohl laid himself down with a pillow of snow for his head, and was presently snoring as tranquilly as if in his own beloved fatherland, with a federbett of the finest down to cover him. The peril of my position prevented me from sleeping. I sat down on a corner of icy rock, and took the liberty of resting my semi-frozen feet on Schlafenwohl's expansive body. I soon began to feel more comfortable. I lighted a pipe (my matches were fortunately in a waterproof case), and anxiously awaited the coming of daylight.

As I sat thus, I began to reflect on my hardness of heart. I had not bestowed a thought on the rest of the passengers, or on the crew, and yet they had probably all perished. But they had met with a sudden and speedy death, whereas I was doomed to a slow and lingering torture. Even supposing that we had a sufficiency of provisions, what prospect of rescue would remain when the last fragment of the iceberg should crumble away under the ceaseless action of the waves? Another and far greater probability was still more appalling. The durability of the iceberg would probably far outlast our store of food. I strove to realise the dreadful situation. Two human beings floating at the caprice of the wind and waves, on a frail deceptive mass of crystallised water, glaring at one another with famine-stricken eyes. At length it would become necessary to cast lots, and decide which should slay the other. Horrible thought! I withdrew my feet hastily from the German's body, and sat, with my head bowed upon my knees, brooding. Exhausted nature yielded, and I fell asleep.

When I awoke, it was broad daylight. At first, I gazed around me with astonishment, as one usually does after sleeping in a strange place, and then proceeded to examine the iceberg. We had been reposing in a small valley, surrounded on every side but the one from which I had entered, by steep rocks of slippery ice, from sixty to eighty feet in height. We were thus completely sheltered from the piercing wind, while even the dash of the breakers was barely distinguishable. I advanced a few paces along the path of ingress, for the purpose of viewing the ocean, and there found Schlafenwohl ensconced in a corner, industriously combing out his flaxen beard, by the aid of a pocket mirror stuck in a crevice of the icy rocks. He was singing *Kenst du das Land*, and saluted me with cheerful calmness.

We breakfasted on a couple of sardines and half a biscuit, slaking our thirst at one of the numerous rills that trickled down the slowly melting rocks. There was something alarming in the idea of thus making a beverage of the house we lived in. Every gallon of water that welled away, represented some six cubic inches of our fragile habitation. If this lique-faction took place in those high southern latitudes, with the temperature scarcely over forty degrees, how rapidly would our floating ark dissolve as we approached the line! If, on the other hand, we drifted antarctically, we ran the risk of being hopelessly frozen up, in regions far beyond the haunts of any human creature. These terrible reflections passed through my mind while I was manufacturing, with the assistance of a pocketknife and the lid of a deal box, a pair of sandals to protect my feet from the chilling surface of the ice. This task completed, I proposed to Schlafenwohl that we should ascend the rocks for the purpose of further ascertaining the extent of the iceberg. He assented, and, after two hours' hard work, principally spent in cutting steps for our feet with our knives, we gained the summit.

The panorama was grand in the extreme. We were full three hundred feet above the surface of the sea, which extended in every direction around us, studded at intervals with icebergs of every imaginable shape and size. Our own island was about a mile in circumference, and presented a series of ridges and valleys, at irregular distances. We stood, as it were, in the centre of a gigantic starfish, whose seven rays were represented by seven rocky backbones, between each of which lay a deep and sheltered valley. The wind blew with great violence at the exposed point where we stood, and, as I have not a remarkably steady head, I did not care to venture too near the edge of any one of the seven abysses below. But the German insisted on it.

'Mr Monkhouse,' said he, 'I vish you vould look over into our valley.'

'Why?'

'I tink somebody, in our absence, may be plondering our prog-box.'

'Nonsense!' I answered. 'You talk as if you were on the top of the Righi.'[38]

'Vell, my friend, you vill oblige me by doing it. I am too stout to venture.'

I crawled on my hands and knees until my face hung immediately over a perpendicular descent of three hundred feet. To my astonishment, I beheld two human figures actively engaged in examining the contents of our invaluable chest.

I reported progress to Schlafenwohl, who became frightfully agitated. He gave vent to sundry Teutonic imprecations, and descended the face of the cliff in the most reckless manner, reaching the bottom some seconds before myself.

When I arrived, I heard voices engaged in loud altercation.

'Vy, you Tom Vite, you are no better dan a tief. Dat is my box.'

'That ain't your private bread,' replied Tom, holding up a biscuit. 'That's ship bread. Ain't it, Bill Atkins?'

'Aye,' said Atkins. 'Besides, you'd never go for to keep all this tucker[39] to your own cheek. Why, there's a parcel of women and children in the next hollow to this, as has had no breakfast yet.'

'What! More people saved?' I exclaimed.

'Of course there is,' said Tom; 'when the iceberg drifted alongside, me and Bill here stood on the bulwarks[40] as the ship heeled over, and passed the passengers in as nicely as if we was off Blackwall Pier.[41] There may be a lot more, for aught I know, in the t'other walleys. I've been busy navigating the ship.'

'Navigating de sheep!' cried Schlafenwohl, 'vot do you mean?'

'Why, I've got a pocket compass here, and I've been heaving the log,' said Tom. 'We're steering nor'-east-and-by-north, and going thirteen knots. If this breeze lasts four-and-twenty hours, we shall go smack into the Falkland Islands.'

'What has become of the skipper, Tom,' I asked, 'and of the other officers?'

'I don't know,' answered Tom; 'they may be aboard the berg, and they mayn't. Anyway, I'm the only able seaman in her that I know of, so I've took the command.'

The adventures of the last few hours had altered Tom White considerably for the better. From a grumbling sulking discontented fellow, he had been transformed into a smart active energetic commander. I verily believe he looked upon the iceberg as an actual ship, and so – barring masts, sails, and rudder – she was.

'Now, Mr Monkhouse,' continued Tom, 'you'll please take your orders from me. I can see you're a sharp chap, by the way you've made them ice shoes and cut them steps in the rock face. Go up to the mast-head, and see what you can make of the other valleys. The next one to this, I know all about; that's my headquarters.'

'Ay, ay, sir,' I replied, in true nautical style, and once more clambered the rocks. I invited Schlafenwohl to accompany me, but he declined. On reaching 'the mast-head,' as Tom styled it, I selected a valley to which the descent was sloping and easy, the sides being deeply covered with snow. Down the surface of this, I glided quite comfortably, and in a few seconds reached the bottom.

At first no human being was visible, but on turning an angle of the cliff, I beheld a singular sight.

Mrs Robinson, the old lady, who on the previous evening had wished that the icebergs would all sink to the bottom in the night-time, and only come up by daylight, was seated crouching on the ground in a state of the utmost terror, holding a large green umbrella over her head. Close beside her reposed an enormous walrus, at least twelve feet long, blinking sleepily at the frightened dame, and looking as little inclined for mischief as a domestic cat on a hearthrug. Laying my finger on my lips to enjoin silence, I fastened a rope (which I had brought with me) round Mrs Robinson's waist, and then proceeded to toil up the slope. I should never have reached the top with her dead weight behind me, but for the umbrella, which I used as an alpenstock.[42] On gaining the summit, Mrs Robinson vowed that she could never go down 'them slippery steps,' so, aided by Bill Atkins, to whom I made signals for assistance, we lowered her safely by a long cable into the women and children's valley.

'Mr Monkhouse,' said Bill, 'we must have that walrus. Even if we can't eat his flesh, we can make a roaring bonfire of his blubber, and the poor women and children are perishing with cold.'

'Ay, ay, sir.'

So, up three or four of us climbed again, armed with knives and cask-staves. We reached the summit and descended into the valley safely. The walrus was seated as placidly as before. He seemed to be making a journey northward to visit some of his Falkland Island acquaintance, and to look upon the iceberg as an admirable species of public conveyance – cheap, swift, and comfortable. He was, however, apparently fonder of the society of ladies than of gentlemen. As soon as he saw us approach, flourishing our weapons, he turned over on his side and quietly rolled into the sea. Our party, chagrined at the cool manner in which he had given us the slip, returned slowly and disconsolately, communicating the result of our proceedings to Tom White.

'Never mind the walrus, boys,' said that energetic commander, who was in high spirits. 'She's going fifteen knots, if she's going an inch. Mr Monkhouse,' he continued, in a whisper, 'you ain't seen the skipper?'

'No, there are no signs of him.'

'Well, if he was aboard, I'd guarantee to bring him in safe. And he couldn't do better nor what I'm doing now.'

What Tom White was doing to assist our progress, it would be hard to say; though he himself firmly believed that everything depended on his exertions.

Evening was coming on. 'Mr Monkhouse,' said Tom, 'you're the best hand I've got aboard the ship. How do you feel about the legs?'

'Rather stiff.'

'Bill Atkins,' said Tom, 'serve out a tot of grog to Mr Monkhouse. It's very precious liquor, for we've only one bottle aboard; but he deserves a drop.'

I swallowed the proffered refreshment, when Tom said:

'Now, I want you to go aloft again, to look out for land.'

'Ay, ay, sir,' I replied, cheerfully, and clambered up like a chamois.

'Land ho!' I called. My distance from Tom was upwards of three hundred feet; but ice must be an excellent conductor of sound, for I could hear Tom's answer quite distinctly, above the whistling of the wind, and the roaring of the waves.

'Where away?'

'On the weather bow,[43] sir.'

'All right. Stop aloft, and say what it looks like as we get nearer.'

A furious gale was now blowing from sou'-sou'-west, and I was obliged to crouch on my hands and knees, to avoid being hurled into one of the chasms beneath. Our gallant iceberg churned through the dark water at railroad speed, leaving a long white track of foam, miles astern. My fear now was, that, at the rate we were going – which could be little short of twenty miles an hour – we should be dashed on the rocks. To my great joy, as we neared the land, I perceived an extensive opening in the cliffs. I described it as accurately as I could, to the watchful commander below. He presently came aloft, and stood at my side.

'Port Stephen's!' he exclaimed, 'by all that's merciful! It lies in the sou'-west corner of the main island. Now comes the ticklish time. If we touch the rocks on either side, we shall be knocked to splinters.'

The excitement on board the iceberg was intense. I will not attempt to describe it. Just as night fell, we entered the harbour. Had our gallant craft been steered by the most skilful helmsman in the British Navy she could not have kept a better course. Tom White rubbed his hands with delight, and appropriated all the honour and glory to himself. As soon as we were fairly inside the harbour, and under the shelter of the cliffs, the force of the wind abated. Fortunately, too, there was a strong current setting out of the harbour, right in the teeth of the wind. We hove the log, and found she was going five knots; we hove it again, a few minutes later, and she was barely making two knots; in a quarter of an hour from that time, a low grinding noise was heard, and we grounded on an extensive sandbank in the centre of the harbour. We were obliged to remain there patiently during the night, as we had no means of communicating, by signal or otherwise, with the shore. We had matches, but the whole of our available fuel amounted to a deal board or two, and so small a fire would, probably, have attracted no observation. We passed a nervous miserable night, and the poor women and children especially. As the iceberg grated backwards and forwards on the top of the bank, we feared she was going to pieces: but her timbers (to speak metaphorically) were well put together, and she held out bravely until morning.

Never in my life did I feel so glad to see the day dawn. We were unspeakably delighted at about sunrise to observe several boats putting out from the settlement. The people in them had put off (it seemed when they came alongside) from motives of curiosity to visit the iceberg, but were perfectly astonished at finding her freighted with passengers.

The official in charge of the boats said, 'We must observe some discipline in getting the people on board, or we shall have the boats swamped. Where is the captain?'

'I am the captain,' quoth Tom White, boldly.

'Then, sir, perhaps you will have the kindness to arrange your people in detachments.'

'Tom bustled about with great pomp, looking fully two inches taller after having been called 'Sir,' and having been addressed so politely by the government officer.

By this time more boats had arrived from shore, and the scanty population of the port were to be seen running to and fro like ants whose nest had been disturbed.

'Are these all your crew and passengers, captain?' asked the governor of the island, as he stepped aboard the iceberg.

'Hall, your worship,' answered Tom, apparently with some indistinct impressions of veneration, derived from the Thames Police Court; 'the others,' he continued solemnly, 'has met a watery grave.'

'Beg your pardon, sir,' said a boatman, touching his cap to Tom White, 'but there's a lot more people, t'other side the berg.'

A rush of boats immediately gave way with a will to the spot indicated, and presently returned, bringing off the captain, chief mate, second mate, third mate, boatswain, doctor, steersman, and midship-men. Being in the afterpart of the ship when the catastrophe occurred, they had all leapt on board the iceberg together. And it seemed that we had searched six valleys, but had omitted to examine the seventh.

Poor Tom White! I believe he was a kind-hearted fellow, and well pleased to find that not a single life had been sacrificed on board the *Golden Dream*; and yet I am sure he was sorry to see the captain again. He spoke not a word on his way to the shore, but hung down his head, and looked much depressed. In the evening, however, under the influence of a liberal libation of grog from His Excellency the Governor, he recovered his spirits, and described his manner of navigating the iceberg into port, in terms that I think no Falkland Islander will ever forget. As for the iceberg, I understand that she remained for many months grounded on the sandbank; at length, under the influence of numerous storms of rain, the ceaseless dashing of the waters, and the warmth of the chilly southern summer, she crumbled to pieces, and disappeared.

We were all placed on board a Californian trader bound for New York. Here, I parted from Schlafenwohl, who had determined to settle in the United States. There was some slight coolness between us. I had positively declined to share the same cabin with him, on account of his snoring, and the worthy German was offended. Consequently, I proceeded to Liverpool by the Cunard steamer from Boston, alone. On reaching London, I at once forwarded a written statement of our extraordinary escape to the Committee at Lloyd's.[44] It was authenticated by Tom White's mark; as he, like many other great men, was unable to read or write. A few days afterwards, I received a requisition to attend before the Committee of Lloyd's, which I at once obeyed, when the following conversation ensued between myself and the Chairman:

'Pray, Mr Monkhouse, is your family of German origin?'

'No, sir; we have been settled for centuries in East Kent.'

'Oh, I beg your pardon; I thought the name of Monkhouse might have been a corruption of the name of a certain Baron, whose extraordinary adventures have long been known to the public.'[45]

HIS BROWN PAPER PARCEL
[by Charles Dickens]

My works are well known. I am a young man in the Art line. You have seen my works many a time, though it's fifty thousand to one if you have seen me. You say you don't want to see me? You say your interest is in my works and not in me? Don't be too sure about that. Stop a bit.

Let us have it down in black and white at the first go off, so that there may be no unpleasantness or wrangling afterwards. And this is looked over by a friend of mine, a ticket writer, that is up to literature. I am a young man in the Art line – in the Fine Art line. You have seen my works over and over again, and you have been curious about me, and you think you have seen me. Now, as a safe rule, you never have seen me, and you never do see me, and you never will see me. I think that's plainly put – and it's what knocks me over.

If there's a blighted public character going, I am the party.

It has been remarked by a certain (or an uncertain) philosopher, that the world knows nothing of its greatest men.[46] He might have put it plainer if he had thrown his eye in my direction. He might have put it, that while the world knows something of them that apparently go in and win, it knows nothing of them that really go in and don't win. There it is again in another form – and that's what knocks me over.

Not that it's only myself that suffers from injustice, but that I am more alive to my own injuries than to any other man's. Being, as I have mentioned, in the Fine Art line, and not the Philanthropic line, I openly admit it. As to company in injury, I have company enough. Who are you passing every day at your Competitive Excruciations? The fortunate candidates whose heads and livers you have turned upside down for life? Not you. You are really passing the Crammers and Coaches. If your principle is right, why don't you turn out tomorrow morning with the keys of your cities on velvet cushions, your musicians playing, and your flags flying, and read addresses to the Crammers and Coaches on your bended knees, beseeching them to come out and govern you? Then, again, as to your public business of all sorts, your Financial statements and your Budgets; the Public knows much, truly, about the real doers of all that! Your Nobles and Right Honourables are first-rate men? Yes, and so is a goose a first-rate bird. But I'll tell you this about the goose; – you'll find his natural flavour disappointing, without stuffing.

Perhaps I am soured by not being popular? But suppose I AM popular. Suppose my works never fail to attract. Suppose that whether they are exhibited by natural light or by artificial, they invariably draw the public. Then no doubt they are preserved in some Collection? No they are not; they are not preserved in any Collection. Copyright? No, nor yet copyright. Anyhow they must be somewhere? Wrong again, for they are often nowhere.

Says you, 'At all events you are in a moody state of mind, my friend.' My answer is, I have described myself as a public character with a blight upon him – which fully accounts for the curdling of the milk in *that* coconut.

Those that are acquainted with London, are aware of a locality on the Surrey side of the river Thames, called the Obelisk, or more generally, the Obstacle. Those that are not acquainted with London, will also be aware of it, now that I have named it. My lodging is not far from that locality. I am a young man of that easy disposition, that I lie abed till it's absolutely necessary to get up and earn something, and then I lie abed again till I have spent it.

It was on an occasion when I had had to turn to with a view to victuals, that I found myself walking along the Waterloo-road, one evening after dark, accompanied by an acquaintance and fellow lodger in the gas-fitting way of life. He is very good company, having worked at the theatres, and indeed he has a theatrical turn himself and wishes to be brought out in the character of Othello; but whether on account of his regular work always blacking his face and hands more or less, I cannot say.

'Tom,' he says, 'what a mystery hangs over you!'

'Yes, Mr Click' – the rest of the house generally give him his name, as being first, front, carpeted all over, his own furniture, and if not mahogany, an out-and-out imitation – 'Yes, Mr Click, a mystery does hang over me.'

'Makes you low, you see, don't it?' says he, eyeing me sideways.

'Why yes, Mr Click, there are circumstances connected with it that have,' I yielded to a sigh, 'a lowering effect.'

'Gives you a touch of the misanthrope too, don't it?' says he. 'Well, I'll tell you what. If I was you, I'd shake it off.'

'If I was you, I would, Mr Click; but if you was me, you wouldn't.'

'Ah!' says he, 'there's something in that.'

When we had walked a little further, he took it up again by touching me on the chest.

'You see, Tom, it seems to me as if, in the words of the poet who wrote the domestic drama of the Stranger,[47] you had a silent sorrow there.'

'I have, Mr Click.'

'I hope, Tom,' lowering his voice in a friendly way, 'it isn't coining, or smashing?'[48]

'No, Mr Click. Don't be uneasy.'

'Nor yet forg– ' Mr Click checked himself, and added, 'counterfeiting anything, for instance?'

'No, Mr Click. I am lawfully in the Art line – Fine Art line – but I can say no more.'

'Ah! Under a species of star? A kind of a malignant spell? A sort of a gloomy destiny? A cankerworm pegging away at your vitals in secret, as well as I make it out?' said Mr Click, eyeing me with some admiration.

I told Mr Click that was about it, if we came to particulars; and I thought he appeared rather proud of me.

Our conversation had brought us to a crowd of people, the greater part struggling for a front place from which to see something on the pavement, which proved to be various designs executed in coloured chalks on the pavement stones, lighted by two candles stuck in mud sconces. The subjects consisted of a fine fresh salmon's head and shoulders, supposed to have been recently sent home from the fishmonger's; a moonlight night at sea (in a circle); dead game; scrollwork; the head of a hoary hermit engaged in devout contemplation; the head of a pointer smoking a pipe; and a cherubim, his flesh creased as in infancy, going on a horizontal errand against the wind. All these subjects appeared to me to be exquisitely done.

On his knees on one side of this gallery, a shabby person of modest appearance who shivered dreadfully (though it wasn't at all cold), was engaged in blowing the chalk dust off the moon, toning the outline of the back of the hermit's head with a bit of leather, and fattening the downstroke of a letter or two in the writing. I have forgotten to mention that writing formed a part of the composition, and that it also – as it appeared to me – was exquisitely done. It ran as follows, in fine round characters: 'An honest man is the noblest work of God. 1 2 3 4 5 6 7 8 9 0. £ s. d. Employment in an office is humbly requested. Honour the Queen. Hunger is a 0 9 8 7 6 5 4 3 2 1 sharp thorn. Chip chop, cherry chop, fol de rol de ri do. Astronomy and mathematics. I do this to support my family.'

Murmurs of admiration at the exceeding beauty of this performance went about among the crowd. The artist having finished his touching (and having spoilt those places), took his seat on the pavement with his knees crouched up very nigh his chin; and halfpence began to rattle in.

'A pity to see a man of that talent brought so low; ain't it?' said one of the crowd to me.

'What he might have done in the coach painting, or house decorating!' said another man, who took up the first speaker because I did not.

'Why he writes – alone – like the Lord Chancellor!' said another man.

'Better,' said another. 'I know *his* writing. *He* couldn't support his family this way.'

Then, a woman noticed the natural fluffiness of the hermit's hair, and another woman, her friend, mentioned of the salmon's gills that you could almost see him gasp. Then, an elderly country gentleman stepped forward and asked the modest man how he executed his work? And the modest man took some scraps of brown paper with colours in 'em out of his pockets and showed them. Then a fair-complexioned donkey with sandy hair and spectacles, asked if the hermit was a portrait? To which the modest man, casting a sorrowful glance upon it, replied that it was, to a certain extent, a recollection of his father. This caused a boy to yelp out, 'Is the Pinter a smoking the pipe, your mother?' who was immediately shoved out of view by a sympathetic carpenter with his basket of tools at his back.

At every fresh question or remark, the crowd leaned forward more eagerly, and dropped the halfpence more freely, and the modest man gathered them up more meekly. At last, another elderly gentleman came to the front, and gave the artist his card, to come to his office tomorrow and get some copying to do. The card was accompanied by sixpence, and the artist was profoundly grateful, and, before he put the card in his hat, read it several times by the light of his candles to fix the address well in his mind, in case he should lose it. The crowd was deeply interested by this last incident, and a man in the second row with a gruff voice, growled to the artist, 'You've got a chance in life now, ain't you?' The artist answered (sniffing in a very low-spirited way, however), 'I'm thankful to hope so.' Upon which there was a general chorus of '*You* are all right,' and the halfpence slackened very decidedly.

I felt myself pulled away by the arm, and Mr Click and I stood alone at the corner of the next crossing.

'Why, Tom,' said Mr Click, 'what a horrid expression of face you've got!'

'Have I?' says I.

'Have you?' says Mr Click. 'Why you looked as if you would have his blood.'

'Whose blood?'

'The artist's.'

'The artist's!' I repeated. And I laughed, frantically, wildly, gloomily, incoherently, disagreeably. I am sensible that I did. I know I did.

Mr Click stared at me in a scared sort of a way, but said nothing until we had walked a street's length. He then stopped short, and said, with excitement on the part of his forefinger:

'Thomas, I find it necessary to be plain with you. I don't like the envious man. I have identified the cankerworm that's pegging away at *your* vitals, and it's envy, Thomas.'

'Is it?' says I.

'Yes, it is,' says he. 'Thomas, beware of envy. It is the green-eyed monster that never did and never will improve each shining hour, but quite the reverse. I dread the envious man, Thomas. I confess that I am afraid of the envious man, when he is so envious as you are. Whilst you contemplated the works of a gifted rival, and whilst you heard that rival's praises, and especially whilst you met his humble glance as he put that card away, your countenance was so malevolent as to be terrific. Thomas, I have heard of the envy of them that follows that Fine Art line, but I never believed it could be what yours is. I wish you well, but I take my leave of you. And if you should ever get into trouble through knifing – or say, garotting[49] – a brother artist, as I believe you will, don't call me to character, Thomas, or I shall be forced to injure your case.'

Mr Click parted from me with those words, and we broke off our acquaintance.

I became enamoured. Her name was Henerietta. Contending with my easy disposition, I frequently got up to go after her. She also dwelt in the neighbourhood of the Obstacle, and I did fondly hope that no other would interpose in the way of our union.

To say that Henerietta was volatile, is but to say that she was woman. To say that she was in the bonnet-trimming, is feebly to express the taste that reigned predominant in her own.

She consented to walk with me. Let me do her the justice to say that she did so upon trial. 'I am not,' said Henerietta, 'as yet prepared to regard you, Thomas, in any other light than as a friend; but as a friend I am willing to walk with you, on the understanding that softer sentiments may flow.'

We walked.

Under the influence of Henerietta's beguilements, I now got out of bed daily. I pursued my calling with an industry before unknown, and it cannot fail to have been observed at that period, by those most familiar with the streets of London, that there was a larger supply – but hold! The time is not yet come!

One evening in October, I was walking with Henerietta, enjoying the cool breezes wafted over Vauxhall Bridge. After several slow turns, Henerietta gaped frequently (so inseparable from woman is the love of excitement), and said, 'Let's go home by Grosvenor-place, Piccadilly, and Waterloo' – localities, I may state for the information of the stranger and the foreigner, well known in London, and the last a Bridge.

'No. Not by Piccadilly, Henerietta,' said I.

'And why not Piccadilly, for goodness' sake?' said Henerietta.

Could I tell her? Could I confess to the gloomy presentiment that overshadowed me? Could I make myself intelligible to her? No.

'I don't like Piccadilly, Henerietta.'

'But I do,' said she. 'It's dark now, and the long rows of lamps in Piccadilly after dark are beautiful. I *will* go to Piccadilly!'

Of course we went. It was a pleasant night, and there were numbers of people in the streets. It was a brisk night, but not too cold, and not damp. Let me darkly observe, it was the best of all nights – FOR THE PURPOSE.

As we passed the garden wall of the Royal Palace, going up Grosvenor-place, Henerietta murmured,

'I wish I was a Queen!'

'Why so, Henerietta?'

'I would make *you* Something,' said she, and crossed her two hands on my arm, and turned away her head.

Judging from this that the softer sentiments alluded to above had begun to flow, I adapted my conduct to that belief. Thus happily we passed on into the detested thoroughfare of Piccadilly. On the right of that thoroughfare is a row of trees, the railing of the Green Park, and a fine broad eligible piece of pavement.

'O my!' cried Henerietta, presently. 'There's been an accident!'

I looked to the left, and said, 'Where, Henerietta?'

'Not there, stupid,' said she. 'Over by the Park railings. Where the crowd is! O no, it's not an accident, it's something else to look at! What's them lights?'

She referred to two lights twinkling low amongst the legs of the assemblage: two candles on the pavement.

'O do come along!' cried Henerietta, skipping across the road with me; – I hung back, but in vain. 'Do let's look!'

Again, designs upon the pavement. Centre compartment, Mount Vesuvius going it (in a circle), supported by four oval compartments, severally representing a ship in heavy weather, a shoulder of mutton attended by two cucumbers, a golden harvest with distant cottage of proprietor, and a knife and fork after nature; above the centre compartment a bunch of grapes, and over the whole a rainbow. The whole, as it appeared to me, exquisitely done.

The person in attendance on these works of art was in all respects, shabbiness excepted, unlike the former person. His whole appearance and manner denoted briskness. Though threadbare, he expressed to the crowd that poverty had not subdued his spirit or tinged with any sense of shame this honest effort to turn his talents to some account. The writing that formed a part of his composition was conceived in a similarly cheerful tone. It breathed the following sentiments: 'The writer is poor but not despondent. To a British 1 2 3 4 5 6 7 8 9 0 Public he £ s. d. appeals. Honour to our brave Army! And also 0 9 8 7 6 5 4 3 2 1 to our gallant Navy. BRITONS STRIKE the A B C D E F G writer in common chalks would be grateful for any suitable employment HOME! HURRAH!' The whole of this writing appeared to me to be exquisitely done.

But this man, in one respect like the last, though seemingly hard at it with a great show of brown paper and rubbers, was only really fattening the downstroke of a letter here and there, or blowing the loose chalk off the rainbow, or toning the outside edge of the shoulder of mutton. Though he did this with the greatest confidence, he did it (as it struck me) in so ignorant a manner, and so spoilt everything he touched, that when he began upon the purple smoke from the chimney of the distant cottage of the proprietor of the golden harvest (which smoke was beautifully soft), I found myself saying aloud, without considering of it:

'Let that alone, will you?'

'Halloa!' said the man next me in the crowd, jerking me roughly from him with his elbow, 'why didn't you send a telegram? If we had known you was coming, we'd have provided something better for you. You understand the man's work better than he does himself, don't you? Have you made your will? You're too clever to live long.'

'Don't be hard upon the gentleman, sir,' said the person in attendance on the works of art, with a twinkle in his eye as he looked at me, 'he may chance to be an artist himself. If so, sir, he will have a fellow feeling with me, sir, when I' – he adapted his action to his words as he went on, and gave a smart slap of his hands between each touch, working himself all the time about and about the composition – 'when I lighten the bloom of my grapes – shade off the orange in my rainbow – dot the i of my Britons – throw a yellow light into my cow-cum-*ber* – insinuate another morsel of fat into my shoulder of mutton – dart another zigzag flash of lightning at my ship in distress!'

He seemed to do this so neatly, and was so nimble about it, that the halfpence came flying in.

'Thanks, generous public, thanks!' said the professor. 'You will stimulate me to further exertions. My name will be found in the list of British Painters yet. I shall do better than this, with encouragement. I shall indeed.'

'You never can do better than that bunch of grapes,' said Henerietta. 'O, Thomas, them grapes!'

'Not better than *that*, lady? I hope for the time when I shall paint anything but your own bright eyes and lips, equal to life.'

'(Thomas did you ever?) But it must take a long time, sir,' said Henerietta, blushing, 'to paint equal to that.'

'I was prenticed to it, Miss,' said the young man, smartly touching up the composition – 'prenticed to it in the caves of Spain and Portingale, ever so long and two year over.'

There was a laugh from the crowd; and a new man who had worked himself in next me, said, 'He's a smart chap, too; ain't he?'

'And what a eye!' exclaimed Henerietta, softly.

'Ah! He need have a eye,' said the man.

'Ah! He just need,' was murmured among the crowd.

'He couldn't come that 'ere burning mountain without a eye,' said the man. He had got himself accepted as an authority, somehow, and everybody looked at his finger as it pointed out Vesuvius. 'To come that effect in a general illumination, would require a eye; but to come it with two dips – why it's enough to blind him!'

That impostor pretending not to have heard what was said, now winked to any extent with both eyes at once, as if the strain upon his sight was too much, and threw back his long hair – it was very long – as if to cool his fevered brow. I was watching him doing it, when Henerietta suddenly whispered, 'Oh, Thomas, how horrid you look!' and pulled me out by the arm.

Remembering Mr Click's words, I was confused when I retorted, 'What do you mean by horrid?'

'Oh gracious! Why, you looked,' said Henerietta, 'as if you would have his blood.'

I was going to answer, 'So I would, for twopence – from his nose,' when I checked myself and remained silent.

We returned home in silence. Every step of the way, the softer sentiments that had flowed, ebbed twenty mile an hour. Adapting my conduct to the ebbing, as I had done to the flowing, I let my arm drop limp, so as she could scarcely keep hold of it, and I wished her such a cold goodnight at parting, that I keep within the bounds of truth when I characterise it as a Rasper.[50]

In the course of the next day, I received the following document:

Henerietta informs Thomas that my eyes are open to you. I must ever wish you well, but walking and us is separated by an unfarmable abyss. One so malignant to superiority – Oh that look at him! – can never never conduct

HENERIETTA

P.S. – To the altar.

Yielding to the easiness of my disposition, I went to bed for a week, after receiving this letter. During the whole of such time, London was bereft of the usual fruits of my labour. When I resumed it, I found that Henerietta was married to the artist of Piccadilly.

Did I say to the artist? What fell words were those, expressive of what a galling hollowness, of what a bitter mockery! I – I – I – am the artist. I was the real artist of Piccadilly, I was the real artist of the Waterloo-road, I am the only artist of all those pavement subjects which daily and nightly arouse your admiration. I do 'em, and I let 'em out. The man you behold with the papers of chalks and the rubbers, touching up the downstrokes of the writing and shading off the salmon, the man you give the credit to, the man you give the money to, hires – yes! and I live to tell it! – hires those works of art of me, and brings nothing to 'em but the candles.

Such is genius in a commercial country. I am not up to the shivering, I am not up to the liveliness, I am not up to the-wanting-employment-in-an-office move; I am only up to originating and executing the work.

In consequence of which you never see me, you think you see me when you see somebody else, and that somebody else is a mere Commercial character. The one seen by self and Mr Click in the Waterloo-road, can only write a single word, and that I taught him, and it's MULTIPLICATION – which you may see him execute upside down, because he can't do it the natural way. The one seen by self and Henerietta by the Green Park railings, can just smear into existence the two ends of a rainbow, with his cuff and a rubber – if very hard put upon making a show – but he could no more come the arch of the rainbow, to save his life, than he could come the moonlight, fish, volcano, ship-wreck, mutton, hermit, or any of my most celebrated effects.

To conclude as I began; if there's a blighted public character going, I am the party. And often as you have seen, do see, and will see, my Works, it's fifty thousand to one if you'll ever see me, unless, when the candles are burnt down and the Commercial character is gone, you should happen to notice a neglected young man perseveringly rubbing out the last traces of the pictures, so that nobody can renew the same. That's me.

HIS PORTMANTEAU
[by Julia Cecilia Stretton]

I

Mr Blorage walked up and down his dining room, on the 31st of December, 1851, with the air and step of a man at peace with the world, and pleased with himself. As he turned to and fro, there was a little swing of exultation in his gait, which no friend (had there been any friend present to witness it) would have recognised as a trait peculiar to Mr Blorage. On the contrary, he passed among his neighbours and acquaintance as a man of a modest and sedate temperament, and of an extreme good nature: so that those same friends and neighbours, full of the impudence of the world, often laughed at the former, and let no opportunity slip of taking advantage of the latter. But he was accustomed to be imposed upon. In fact, it was his business, his vocation, to which he had been apprenticed from his earliest childhood.

It is recorded by his nurse and mother, that so amiable, so complacent a baby never was born. A faint whimper was the only complaint he made, after lying for hours in his cradle wide awake, with nothing but a damaged tassel to amuse him, as it swung to and fro from the hood of the cradle in the draught – which draught reddened his baby nose, and brought the water into his little weak eyes. As he grew up, it became an established fact, that Master Dick was to be washed first or last, taken out or left behind, given sugarplums or forgotten, as it happened to suit the peculiar fancy of every other person rather than Master Dick himself, because he was so sweet tempered. Thus he weathered babyhood, encountered childhood, and rushed up into boyhood, in a pleasing and satisfactory manner to all parties, himself included. He never worried his mother by catching infectious diseases at wrong times; he went through the necessary ailments of childhood – such as measles, whooping cough, and scarlatina – with the least possible degree of trouble to all parties concerned; and caused no anxiety by having relapses, or taking colds. If he cut his finger to the bone, no one knew of it, unless anyone chanced to notice the scar. If he fell into the river, he scrambled out, and dried his own clothes, by the convenient process of airing them on his own body. If he fell off a tree, down a well, over a wall, he picked himself up and bore his burden of bruises with silent composure. In addition to these accomplishments, he bore any amount of other people's work, and seemed rather to enjoy being 'put upon.' He was glad to be obliging, and 'gave up' with quite as much zest as other natures about him delighted to 'take all.' Once, and once only, did a slight attack of ill temper and discontent assail him. His father, without any previous notice, without the shadow of a consultation as to any faint bias on Dick's part, but just because 'he was Dick, and would be sure to do it, whether he liked it or not,' placed him, at the age of sixteen years, as the junior of all the junior clerks, in a Bank.

Now, Dick was a country boy, born and brought up in truly rural fashion. His father having a small estate, farmed the greater part of it himself, and, being a practical man, did nothing by halves. His children participated in all that he did, as much for their own benefit as for his. The boys were active young farmers from the time they were breeched; and the girls reared chickens, and understood the immaculate cleanliness of a dairy, before they could spell their own names. So Dick's habits, and what little idiosyncrasy he had of his own, belonged wholly to the country.

He was up with the lark, roaming over his father's premises, and lighting upon all sorts of charitable things to do. A brood of young ducks, always erratic, obstinate, and greedy, had squeezed their mucilaginous little bodies through nothing, and were out on the loose, their vigilant foster mother, 'in a fine frenzy,' clacking within the shut-up poultry house. It was Dick's business to open the door and give her lost ones to her cherishing wings; and all the acknowledgement he got was an unmistakable indication on the part of the irritated mother that he alone had been the cause of the separation. He delighted to stagger under a load of fodder, taking, as high and invaluable wages, the glad neigh of the expectant horse, or the gentle soft low of the cow. He rushed into the matitutinal quarrel of the bantam-cock and the great bubbley-jock; he coaxed with crumbs of bread the shy little pullets, and covertly threw handfuls of grain to the ostracised cockerels, who dared not so much as look upon a crumb within sight of the proud monarch of the poultry yard.

Having meddled and messed in everything that was going on, to the high delight of himself, if of nothing else, Dick would return to the house, brush and clean himself with scrupulous exactness, and place himself ready to receive his mother's morning kiss on his cool rosy soap-shining cheeks. After that, he began the real business of the day; he nursed the baby, made the tea, cut the bread and butter, administered it, adjusted quarrels, ran the messages, and took what breakfast he could between whiles. When he had a few moments he could call his own, he roamed about, saving young birds from remorseless kidnappers, rescuing puppies and kittens from untimely fates, helping little maidens over high stiles, and assisting old women to carry faggots of sticks, assuredly stolen from his father's hedgerows.

Dick possessed one harmless propensity – never to see a hill without paying it the compliment of running to the top of it in so many minutes, and speeding down to the bottom again in so many minutes less. He considered it a duty he owed to society at large, to be able to say in how short a time society could approach so much nearer to heaven.

For these reasons, and a thousand more such, Dick's dismay may be comprehended when he was suddenly required to exchange breezy hilltops and flowery plains, for the high stool, matching the higher desk, in a dusty cloudy cobwebby back Bank office, in a close dull unsavoury street.

Dick began a remonstrance. For the first time in his life, there rose to his lips the murmur of a complaint. The person upon whose ear the unwonted sound fell, was his younger brother: called William by his godfathers and godmothers, Bill by those who had no particular regard for him, or he for them, and Billy by the fortunate possessors of what affections he had. Generally obtuse to everything that did not concern himself, he was visibly startled by the unwonted moan, and kindly said, under the shock of surprise:

'Come, come, old fellow! None of that.'

'But I don't like the Bank, Billy. I am unhappy; I think I am dreadfully unhappy; the smell of the place makes me sick; I get the cramp in my legs from sitting on that high stool; I am as nervous – '

'Hold hard, Dick; I won't have you say another word. How dare you talk like that to me?'

'My dear Billy – '

'Don't dear Billy me. When you know as well as I do, that if you don't stay at the Bank *I* shall have to go there!'

'Oh dear!' ejaculated Dick.

'Oh dear!' mimicked the fast younger brother. 'I wonder you have the heart to hint an objection, Dick – especially knowing, as you do, how you hate the Bank. Endangering your own brother! And you setting up for being a good-natured fellow, too!'

Dick said no more, but manfully bore up against smells, cramps, nerves, and headaches, with the mental comfort and consolation, 'How lucky poor dear Billy is saved all this!'

Time worked its own cure, and he experienced in his own person the truth of that well-established maxim, 'Habit becomes second nature.' He exercised his peculiar vocation by doing a great deal of other people's work besides his own; by cherishing solitary and forlorn-looking spiders; assisting flies out of a persistent search into ink bottles; and being generally kind-hearted to everything and everybody.

He was universally liked, though vastly imposed upon; still, upon his gradual elevation, in course of time, from junior of the juniors to head of all, there was no voice but his own that hazarded a doubt on the fitness of the election. He was a little uncomfortable himself lest he should have taken a place one of the others might have coveted or better deserved.

At last assured that his abilities and position warranted the choice, Dick resigned himself to being entirely happy, and – as a fall essential to a state of bliss – fell in love.

That his choice should light on one profoundly unlike himself, was perfectly natural; a young lady of much beauty and many wants being exactly the being to appear angelic in Dick's eyes. Had she been possessed of brains, or of sufficient capacity to see into the depths of Dick's most honest heart, she might have ruled there, queen and wife, and her domestic kingdom would have ennobled her in all eyes; but, like a playful kitten, incipient cruelty lurked in her prettiest ways. Her character may be inferred from the answer she gave Dick when he tendered her his all.

'Indeed, Mr Richard, you are very good! How you have surprised me! And do you really think so well of me? I never thought you really cared a bit for me. I laughed and chatted with you, because, as we all said, Mr Richard Blorage was so good natured.'

'Good natured to *you*, Ellen! Oh, Heaven, could you read nothing more in my devotion? Not the deepest, strongest, most enduring love?'

'You quite amaze me, Mr Richard! Where have you kept these feelings so long?'

'Oh, Ellen! Do not trifle with me!'

'No! Not for worlds, Mr Blorage! I am no flirt. I am a frank creature, and always will be.'

'I thought – I hoped – oh, Ellen! I would not have dared to speak thus, and lay bare my heart before you, had you not encouraged – '

'Now, Mr Richard, don't say that, I beg! I am sure I am above that. Besides, mamma wishes me to marry rather high. She wishes me to set my younger sisters a good example; and indeed papa has said to me more than once, that he would never suffer me to marry a banker's clerk.'

'I am to be a partner in two years.'

'Two years! I may be married long before that. Come, Mr Richard, don't be cast down. We can always be the best of friends.'

'And my wife, Ellen?'

'Oh dear no! I really wonder you could ever think of such a thing – so good natured, as you are. Pray don't tease me any more.'

Poor Dick's tender heart swelled and throbbed with many tender emotions; but he really was too good natured to let any angry or bitter thoughts divide it. He rallied his fluttering and bewildered senses, looked round for his hat (an article that always seems of great comfort to Englishmen in difficulties), looked into it, and not finding a single word in it to help him out, went away speechless with a single bow. It was a bow worthy of Sir Charles Grandison,[51] and it was a far more natural bow than Sir Charles Grandison ever made. There was a quiet dignity in it, expressive of so much integrity and worth, that it even smote the little silly substitute for a heart that had so mocked him, with a stab of misgiving.

Time, that never-failing plaster that heals so many wounds, came to Dick's aid. He derived a melancholy satisfaction from working twice as hard as he had ever done before. He was at that once odious office before the doors were opened, and sat on his high stool for hours at a stretch, regardless of cramp. From always being a compassionate and good-natured fellow, he became morbidly so: appearing to regard the whole of his acquaintance as victims to unrequited love, upon whom it was essential he should expend a vigilant care of the most forbearing and affectionate nature.

Not even the fast, worldly-wise opinion of William, Bill, or Billy, could make him think he was an ill-used man.

'She's a flirt, and no mistake. *I* saw through her long ago, Dick. I always said she would jilt you.'

'You wrong her, William – you deeply wrong her. She was right in her decision. She deserved a better fate than to be the wife of a banker's clerk.'

'Pooh, pooh! Ha, ha! Why, you have a share in the firm already, and may call yourself banker at once, and I hope to the Lord you will soon get rich. It will be devilish comfortable, Dick, always to be able to turn to you when one wants five or ten pounds.'

'Do you want a little money now, Billy? I have no occasion to hoard money.'

'The very thing I do want, my dear fellow. I never was so hard up. I say! It's a great comfort to me, Dick, that you didn't marry that simpleton of a girl.'

'Hush, Bill.'

'Well, it's a very good thing for yourself, then. I'll swear she was a screw.'

'Forbear, Bill.'

'Well, it was an uncommon good thing for her, then.'

'That is my only consolation,' sighed the good Dick, as he handed his brother a bundle of notes, which, true to business habits, he carefully counted over twice.

'Twenty-five pounds; thank ye, Dick.'

II

Bless us! Mr Blorage has been a long time walking up and down that dining room of his.

Had the volatile Ellen at last relented, that he walked up and down with that elastic step? No, no. She had married within six months of blighting Dick – had married an Honourable by name, if not by nature; but the title being of much more consequence than the fact, there is no need to enquire further. If Dick's prayers could make her happy, she was supremely blest.

No. Mr Blorage was excited, because he was dining in his own new, substantially built, elegantly furnished, luxuriously ornamented, house – a house that had been pronounced perfect – a gem of a house – a house that only wanted one more thing, to be absolute perfection. He was dining in it, for the first time, and he had (though naturally a sober man), under the pressure of such an extreme circumstance, drank success to it, and health to himself, just about once too often. Hence, thought was running riot in his brain, like an express engine gone mad. Here was he, at the good and pleasant age of thirty-five, an independent gentleman, with fifteen hundred a year, honestly made, and safely deposited in the only bank that never breaks – her Majesty's Consols.[52] Besides, he still held a lucrative and independent position in the very Bank once so disagreeable to him. He was not a responsible partner, he was only the trusted confidential manager. 'For, as to partnerships,' thought Dick, 'it would never do for me to lose my money through the speculations of others. I could not help Billy, or send little Maude to that first-rate London school. As to my dear mother, Old Grobus' legacy (I wonder why he left it to me?) just fell in, in time to make her comfortable.'

Dick had grown rich, nobody quite knew how. As he was always helping everyone, perhaps he realised the promise, 'Cast thy bread upon the waters, and it shall return unto thee a hundredfold.' He had made one or two fortunate speculations. He had been left a legacy by old Grobus, a morose brother clerk, who had never given him a civil word when alive, but had bequeathed him all he died worth, remarking in his will that 'Richard Blorage, his heir, would be sure to spend it better than he could.' And Richard Blorage, first ascertaining that there were no real heirs, had forthwith purchased one or two waste bits of land, because the owners wanted to sell them, and because no one but a good-natured fool would buy them. No sooner, however, did they become Dick's than they were discovered to be invaluable. The railway ran straight through them; the land was the very thing for building purposes; and what was pleasanter than all, no one envied Dick. Everyone said, 'Serve Dick Blorage right; he's a good fellow, and it's his due.'

And when he decided to build himself a new house on this improved and flourishing estate, everyone, far and near, entered into the scheme. The plans were shown about, as if the plans were for a building of public property. The architect was received everywhere as a friend, the workmen were looked upon as part of the community. The house grew, stone by stone, under the eyes and minute inspection of all the neighbours. The laying of the foundation stone was a popular jubilee; the roofing-in was nearly followed by a roofing-out, so deafening were the cheers from the assembled multitude. The final completion of the structure was so rapturously hailed by all Dick's friends, that it might have been supposed Mr Blorage had privately intimated to the whole of them, individually and separately, that he intended to make each a present of the achieved piece of architecture.

Of course there was to be a house-warming – a dinner and a dance; and it was thinking of this identical fête, to come off the very next day, that had set Mr Blorage's thoughts off at express pace. Not because his dinner was to be so well appointed, not because his wines (he knew that a little too well this evening!) were unexceptionable, not because the music provided was the best that money could hire, not because his rooms were beautifully decorated, his chintzes of the sweetest patterns, his carpets Axminster and Brussels; but because two out of the sixty invitations he had issued had been accepted. Why two? And what two? In the present excited state of Mr Blorage's brain, he could only have answered, 'Upon those two hangs my fate – the fate of my house.'

He threw himself into one of those delightful spring-seated sloping-backed softly cushioned armchairs, in which our unlucky ancestors never had the good fortune to repose. He took another glass of wine, oblivious of having drank success to his house already rather often.

'So, they both come! Lovely creatures! Bill doesn't like Fanny; he says she is like Ellen. Ah, poor Ellen. I don't know which is the prettier of those two cousins. Billy seems rather full of Florence. I must find that out; I must observe him; it would never do to ruin poor Bill's happiness; I know what unrequited love is. I am not in love with either of the cousins at present. I was madly in love with Ellen, but, you see, I got over it.' (Who was there to see Mr Blorage? Ah, that last glass!) 'It certainly is time I married. But I shouldn't like to be served that way again – as Ellen served me, I mean. Bill will have it she's unhappy; I hope not. Bill says I am a great fool if I ever – if I submit – if, in short, I am taken in again. Did Ellen take me in? I don't know. I don't understand women at all. I believe every word they say; I adore their sweet smiles and winning ways, and I would not – nay, I could not – think ill of them for the world. I suppose I am a fool, as Bill says I am. What a thing it would be for me if some kind-hearted honest genius, or fairy, would bestow upon the walls of my house the gift of making people appear just as they are, speak just what they think, and be altogether as God and Nature made them! When I was young, surely I read of a palace of truth belonging to some fellow – king, I beg his pardon – called Phanor.[53] To be sure, they got into a world of difficulties, and were all more or less miserable. But they were French people; whereas a good honest Briton likes the truth, and WILL speak it whether he's miserable or not.'

Mr Blorage spoke the last sentence aloud, with great emphasis on the auxiliary verb; moreover, giving force to his words by an energetic thump on the arm of his chair.

'My dear sir, take care!' said a voice in his ear. The sound was like the tinkle of a little silver bell, clear as a note of music.

Looking towards the sound, the good Dick perceived, perched on the arm of the chair, a little lady: who steadied herself, after his hard thump on the cushion, by holding valiantly on to an elaborately crocheted antimacassar.

'I – I beg your pardon,' stammered Mr Blorage.

'Granted,' said the lady. 'Now, open your hand, and hold it steady.'

Always ready to oblige, Mr Blorage did as he was asked, and was wonderfully surprised that he was *not* surprised when she took a flying leap into the middle of his palm.

'Thank you, Dick,' said she, arranging her little crinoline, and putting on an air. 'So you want your house to be gifted with the power of making people speak the truth, eh?'

'I should like it,' he answered, in some confusion.

The little lady shook her head.

'You won't like it. You will find it very annoying. Neither your servants, nor your friends, nor your relations, will seem the better for it, Dick.'

'I should like to try it for a little while – just for one day,' he stammered, in answer to the wise forebodings of the little lady.

'I understand. Merely to enable you to select a wife? You fear to be made a fool of again, Dick.'

'Yes, yes,' he answered, eagerly. 'Marriage is such an awful thing. One does not mind being made a fool of for a short time – but for life!' Dick shuddered, and the little lady was nearly upset by the shock.

In the endeavour to save herself from falling, she unfolded a pair of beautiful wings, whose transparent lustre of prismatic colours formed a sort of Glory round her head.

'How pretty you are,' said Dick.

'I only show my beauty to those who appreciate me. My name is Verita.'

'God bless the name,' said Dick. 'I don't care about the enchantment of my house, if you will always be at hand to advise me.'

'I mean to live with you, Dick; but as for advice, why did God give you an intelligence to guide you through every difficulty? Why ask a little odd spirit for advice, when you have but to knock at the door of your conscience for unerring guidance?'

'True,' murmured Dick; 'but still – '

'I see you hold to your own way, Dick, and as I wish you to have a good wife, I will grant your request. But inasmuch as enchanting the whole house would be extremely inconvenient to you in more ways than one, I will confine the spell to this chair. But there are conditions to be observed – two conditions – before I enchant the chair.'

'Name them.'

'The first is, that no one but yourself is to be apprised of the power the chair possesses.'

'Dear me,' exclaimed Mr Blorage, dubiously, 'would that be quite fair?'

'Simpleton! Who could you get to sit in your chair if its power were known, Dick?'

'Wouldn't people like it? I shouldn't mind.'

'I dare say *you* would not. But assent to the condition, or the chair is not enchanted.'

'I consent. You said, dear madam, there was another condition?'

'The second condition is, that whoever enters within your doors *must* sit in the chair, and *must* answer three questions before leaving the chair.

'But suppose people will do neither the one nor the other?'

'Compliance with the first condition I will take upon myself to ensure; the second depends on you, as it is you who must put the three questions.'

'What sort of questions?'

'Pooh, pooh, Dick, don't give me more than my share of work. If you don't know the sort of questions to put, in order to obtain the good for which you have required me to enchant the chair, you are undeserving of the favour.'

Dick would have protested, but he was so fearful of disturbing the equilibrium of the delicate little creature by over-earnest utterance, that he only opened and shut his mouth.

'Don't blow me away! I must be gone, though. The night is rather chilly, I think.' She took out of an almost invisible pocket, a shadowing sort of cobwebby thing, meant, he presumed, for her handkerchief. Gracefully throwing it over her head, and tying it under her little atom of a chin, she continued: 'Goodnight, Dick. And good fortune to this house! And may it soon possess the only charm it wants – a pretty wife for you, and a good mistress for itself!'

Before Mr Blorage had time to answer, the palm of his hand was empty, and the fair little creature had disappeared.

III

Mr Richard Blorage was never quite clear during how long a time after the spirit's disappearance, he sat thinking or dozing. But the dining-room door having opened and shut several times during this period of intense thought or doze, he at length became conscious that it was not likely to have opened and shut of its own accord, and that it had probably done so under the hand of Penge, his butler, his new butler, the most respectful and obsequious of butlers, who had come into his service with a character so very unexceptionable, that he had almost felt inclined to thank the spotless Penge for being so good as to take him for a master.

Mr Blorage rose hastily and rang the bell. Penge answered it so immediately, as to justify the supposition that when it rang, he had once again had his hand on the doorhandle.

Mr Blorage was about to speak to the excellent Penge, when he was arrested by seeing that modest butler seat himself with much humility in the chair his master had just vacated – the enchanted chair. He was no sooner seated than his appearance instantly changed. His countenance assumed an air of much self-complacency; he drew out from the depths of a mysterious pocket, a snuffbox; and he took a large pinch of snuff in a calm and deliberate manner.

'It is my only vice, sir,' he remarked; 'I trust it is not disagreeable? Will you take a pinch? No ceremony.'

Villains, ruffians, rogues, and fast men, are above being surprised; or, if they do feel any slight attack of that weakness, they take care not to show it. But plain honest natural creatures are constantly surprised, and as constantly show it. Mr Blorage gazed at his butler, open-mouthed and open-eyed, and in the greatest surprise, until he was suddenly recalled to a perception of the case, by seeing the face of the little spirit peeping out behind the chair.

The Lady Verita had performed her part of the contract, and had seated the butler in it by some marvellous power. Mr Blorage must now perform his part of the contract.

As he rubbed his eyes, ran his fingers through his hair, and blew his nose, perfectly unable to decide what questions he should put to Penge, the confident air of the man, shining through an obsequious mock humility, moved Mr Blorage to a hearty and irresistible fit of laughter. Though he was sorry for Penge, though he felt that he alone was to blame for Penge's peculiar situation, restrain himself from laughter he could not.

'Vell, Blorage,' says Penge, with great self-possession, you 'ave a right to amuse yourself at your pleasure; but you're drunk!'

'Penge?'

'Blorage! I ain't to be put out of the truth by you. You're drunk.'

'Drunk or sober, I think I am a gentleman, Penge?'

'*You* may think so,' returned the model butler, with great contempt; 'but *I* don't. *My* ideas of a real gent, ain't by no manner o' means the same as yours, Blorage.'

'And what are your ideas?' asked Dick, in a hurry, glad to catch hold of so safe a question.

'My ideas,' replied the model butler, rising with the occasion, 'are racers – out-and-outers – sport – life. Them's my ideas of a real gentleman, not *your* slow games. Blorage! you're a muff.'

Dick blushed a little, in mortification; but it was clearly his duty to get this, his first victim, out of the chair of truth as speedily as possible.

'At all events, I hope you are comfortable, Penge? I hope that at least you like my service?'

'No, I don't, Blorage. I am formed for enjyment; and how can I know enjyment under a mean-spirited screw that keeps the keys of his own cellar?'

'But you agreed with me, Penge, when I engaged you, that it was the most satisfactory arrangement for all parties. Penge, you said you preferred it.'

'Blorage, I considered as it looked well so to say; and having heerd as you was soft and easy, what I said to myself was, "Penge! you stick that into him, and you'll have the key before your first year is out." Which is what I expect, Blorage, or you and me parts.'

Burning to release the prisoner, Mr Blorage was racking his brain for the last question, when a furious peal of the doorbell suggested a very safe one.

'Who can that be, Penge?'

'That awful young scamp your brother!'

Then, instantly rising, Mr Penge said, in his most unexceptionable manner, 'I ask your pardon, sir. I felt so very giddy just now, sir, that if I had not took the liberty to take a seat, I must have fainted.'

'Never mind. Make no excuses, Penge.'

'Thank you, sir. I believe that is Mr Williams's ring, sir. He is such a cheerful young gentleman, sir, that I know the liveliness of his ring.' And Penge disappeared with alacrity.

The good Dick rushed to the chair, intending to occupy it himself during his brother's visit. But his brother was too quick for him.

'Halloa, Dick! What do you want with the best chair in the room? It is very unlike such a good-natured chap as you to appropriate the most comfortable seat.'

He was in the chair! Dick sat down on the edge of another chair, and wiped his forehead.

William, Billy, or Bill, safely ensconced in the magic chair, assumed a very rakish used-up indifferent sort of appearance; and the brothers were silent. Probably William was uncomfortable in his strange and novel position. Dick was racking his brain for three questions – three simple harmless questions, that should not commit the sitter. The weather? Nothing better. Bill could never compromise himself about the weather.

'Is it a fine night, Billy?'

'Rather too fine for me. I want to skulk off to Barnes's without being seen, and I came here on my way, partly to blind mother, and partly to twist a fi'-pun' note out of you.' (Barnes's was a disreputable gaming place.)

'How is our mother?' interrupted Dick, in a violent hurry.

'Precious cross. Bothering as much about my goings on, as if I was cutting my teeth.'

'Are – are – are you in love, Bill?'

'Yes; with myself. What's the good of loving anything else? I don't find anyone so deuced fond of me as to forget himself or herself.'

'I thought Florence – ' interrupted Dick, hastily.

'Florence be hanged! Do you suppose I don't see that you are spooney upon Florence? But lookee here, Dick; you want to marry; now, I don't intend to let you marry. I'm not going to stand your being thrown away upon any other than your own relations.'

'Come out of that chair, Bill!'

'I won't. It's a comfortable chair. I'm bent on telling you my mind. My mind has been full of you, Dick, ever since you began to build this house. That's a suspicious gallery, shut off by a green baize door. I said when I saw it, that means mischief. He means that part of the house for a Nur – '

'Come out of that chair, Bill!'

'I tell you I won't. As to your getting married, I'm not afraid of Fanny; her temper will never stand a month's courtship. She'll show her teeth in a fortnight. When I turned this matter over in my mind, I said to myself, "Dick is safe from *her*. But Florence," I said, "may be dangerous; therefore I'll pretend to be a little affected that way myself."'

'Here, Bill! Take five pounds – take ten pounds – but come out of that chair!'

'I would have done it for less than that, Dick, but as you are so flush and free of money, I'll take the ten. Good evening, Dick; I promised mother to be back to tea.'

With this sudden change, Mr William took himself out of the chair, and took his leave. Mr Richard – too well pleased to have got him out of the chair, to care for anything more, and knowing that his nerves were incapable of bearing further strain – rushed upstairs and dived into bed. And, as if fearing that the chair would pursue him even there, and entice people to commit themselves, he pulled the bedclothes over his head, and was fortunate in being unconscious during the rest of the night.

HIS HAT BOX
[by Julia Cecilia Stretton]

IV

When Mr Blorage awoke in the morning, he was reminded by a slight headache, that something unusual had occurred; but he came out of his cold bath as lively and fresh and full of spirits as if he were the combined essence of two or three dozen Mr Blorages. He pranced downstairs – his own newly built and Brussels-carpeted stairs – like a young colt philandering in a clover meadow.

This was the great day of the house-warming, to be followed by events that were perfectly bewildering from the ecstasy of their anticipation. He was brought back to a state of common human bliss by a strong smell of burnt wood or varnish, and found that in making the tea (he had lost himself in thinking how soon some fair hand might be making tea for him) he was endeavouring to stuff his little hot kettle (which phizzed and sputtered a remonstrance) into his new teapoy, while the caddy appertaining thereto was catching fire on the hob.

Remedying these mistakes with the utmost expedition, in turning round he suddenly encountered the chair, and suddenly remembered its fatal property.

What was he to do? How get rid of the chair? Should he send it away? Should he lock it up? Should he destroy it? burn it? annihilate it? bury it?

As he seized hold of it, with the intention of performing one or other of these acts, he was conscious of a shock; his arms fell powerless to his sides; and a little fluttering noise made him look up. There, on the head of a chair, was the Lady Verita, her wings expanded, her tiny foot just poised on the carved shining top of the chair.

'It is of no use, Dick,' she said, her little voice tinkling like silver music. 'This chair was not enchanted merely for your whim. Sit down, and listen to me.'

Dick obeyed, and held out his palm. His heart leaped with joy as the little lady sprang lightly on to it.

'Lend me your watch, Dick, to sit upon.'

Dick complied, and placed his watch with infinite care and gentleness for her use.

She seated herself gracefully, having folded her wings. Once more drawing out her fleecy atom of a handkerchief, she used it after the manner of mortals: though Dick hardly supposed that anything so infinitely delicate as her nose could stand the test.

'Now, Dick, how naughty you are! You do not use my gift as you ought. Why were you thinking of burning my chair? Simply because it had done its duty in enabling you to see people as they really are, and know their thoughts?'

'But I do not wish to know them.'

'My dear Dick, infinite wisdom has given you susceptibility, intelligence, and reason. You only use the first. You are commanded to love your neighbour, but your susceptibility should not lead you into confounding all moral distinctions among your neighbours. Reason should step in, and enable you to make a practical use of susceptibility and intelligence. Do I make myself understood? I have had to read up for it.'

'Lovely and beloved little creature, I know I am a fool, but let me reap the fruits of my want of wisdom. I would rather be foolish for life than entrap others into sitting in this chair.'

'Dick, you require a lesson. Use it well, be patient, be submissive, and all will end well, both for you and for me. I hear your doorbell ringing. Adieu, Dick. Be wise and prudent.'

The radiant wings expanded, the little handkerchief was tied under the tiny chin, and, as Penge opened the door to usher in a visitor, the little lady vanished.

'Be wise and prudent.' The words kept tinkling a little silver sound in the ears of Mr Blorage, as he rose and welcomed the visitor shown in by Penge. His first essay at being wise and prudent, made him hand her (for it was a female) at once into the post of honour – the Chair of Truth.

He was glad to perceive that his visitor was a pleasant little mild girl, whom he had met once or twice at Dr Evans', the medical man of the neighbourhood. He had a general idea that she was the daughter of an invalid widow, and that she was the eldest of a flock of brown healthy-looking children, to whom she acted as foster mother, owing to the inability of their real mother to do anything but lie on her sofa, and sigh for ease from pain and poverty.

He had so far noticed little Gatty Bland (who, by the by, was twenty-three years old, perhaps more) as to admire her eyes, soft and brown, the exact colour of her hair. As she now sat in the enchanted chair, he was surprised at himself for never having noticed that she was really pretty. Her sweet innocent face had a bewitching air about it that peculiarly pleased him. And really, her tiny hands and her graceful movements strongly reminded him of the ways of the little Lady Verita.

'Mamma has sent me here this morning, Mr Blorage, to beg your acceptance of the loan of a beautiful china bowl. There is not another like it in England, and she fancied it would be just the thing to hold a Trifle tonight.'

'I thank her very much; but how did she know that I was going to have a Trifle tonight?'

'Oh, we know it very well. You give a ball tonight, and from our house we can see the lights, and faintly hear the music. Jenny and Albert are to sit up tonight a little longer than usual that they may watch the carriages.'

'Then if I accept the loan of the beautiful china bowl, I must ask a favour in return.'

'I will promise to perform it, Mr Blorage, for I feel sure you will not ask anything that I may not promise to perform.'

'I am proud of being so trusted. I should wish to beg the favour of your company tonight, to see how well the Trifle looks in the beautiful china bowl.'

'Ah, how I wish we could come! But we are very poor, and mamma is too great an invalid to take us out. We shall find much pleasure, though, in watching your gaiety from our window, and we shall be delighted to think that our china bowl has helped to ornament your supper table. Mamma was sure you would not consider the offer of it an impertinence.'

No, indeed! Dick was an adept in the happy art of accepting a kindness in the spirit in which it was offered.

'Mamma has had great pleasure in watching the building of your house, Mr Blorage. She said, a good man is going to inhabit it, and a good man always benefits a neighbourhood.'

'Your mamma is very kind,' murmured Dick, a little confused, and beginning to blush. He was admiring Gatty Bland so much, that he had forgotten she was a prisoner, and unconscious of the frankness of her words.

'Mamma is very good, Mr Blorage, as we, her children, know. And I ought to return to her. I promised not to be absent more than half an hour, and it must be that now.'

But though she looked distressed and anxious, poor Gatty could no more move until Mr Blorage released her, than the house could move.

He wiped his brow, ran his fingers through his hair, and prepared for action.

'And so your mamma is glad to have a near neighbour?'

'She is glad that you are our neighbour. When it pleases Heaven to release her from trouble and pain, and to begin our lonelier life of struggle, she thinks that the sunshine of a good man's heart may sometimes fall on her poor children in the shade.'

'So it shall, my dear, please God! But, Gatty, you must marry. – Would you like to marry?'

'I don't know, Mr Blorage; but I fear few will care to marry a little plain girl, with a turn-up nose, and a heart full of her own people, and who wants a nomination for – '

'Have you ever seen anyone you would like to marry?' interrupted Dick, pleased with his wealth of questions.

'Only one, and that is you, Mr Blorage! Goodbye. I must run all the way home.'

Finding herself released, Gatty sprang up, and ran out of the room: leaving Mr Blorage turning from his natural colour to white, from white to pink, from pink to crimson, from crimson to purple.

'Poor little dear thing, that I could have been so base and dishonourable as to ask her such a delicate question, when I had so many safe questions to ask – her age, her brothers' and sisters' names and ages, her godfathers and godmothers – if she liked new milk, cheese, eggs. Gracious Heaven! that I should have dared to put so preposterous a question, and receive such a – such a – such a – ' Dick could not bring himself to name the quality of the answer. 'But it's very pleasant to be so undeservedly appreciated – to be liked and loved for one's own sake. She is a nice little thing; she is a pretty little thing. Her nose certainly turns up; but I believe there never was a silly person known with a turned-up nose. She is very graceful. She flitted out of the room like a bird out of a rosebush. I wonder what nomination she wanted!'

For the first time since it was enchanted, Mr Blorage looked complacently at the chair; but his meditations were interrupted by a respectful intimation from Penge that his master would oblige everybody by getting out of the way, because the market gardener had arrived with his flowers and decorations, the carpenter was waiting with his nails and ruler, and the Mr Gunter of those parts was frantic to begin setting up his lights. So, Mr Blorage got out of the way for the rest of the day, and reappeared at dinnertime in due course, and afterwards became the observed of all observers, as he led out the (in those parts) highly renowned and celebrated Lady Fitzcluck to open his ball with an old-fashioned country dance.

Everything had gone off well, up to the proud moment when Mr Blorage drew on his new kid gloves for the (in those parts) eminently aristocratic Lady Fitzcluck. She was bulky, but she was light in hand, and she and Mr Blorage danced with a spirit worthy of the occasion. Half way down thirty couples, Mr Blorage became conscious of a circumstance. A stately old dowager was seated, in the centre of a circle of chairs, in the Chair of Truth. Howsoever it had got there, by whatsoever mysterious agency it had been brought there, there it was, with the dowager in it. She was encircled by a crowd, to whom she was holding forth, and evidently in no complimentary strain. Mr Blorage rushed out of the country dance at the instance when he ought to have paraded the (in those parts) highly fashionable Lady Fitzcluck down the middle; he rushed back again, and danced vehemently; he grasped the hand confidingly held across to him in the execution of the figure hands across, as if it were the throat of a burglar; in all the hurry, worry, and confusion he must think (and could not think) of three appropriate and respectful questions to put to that terrible and otherwise immovable old dowager. With his responsibility staring him in the face, he had hurled Lady Fitzcluck through a narrow gorge of dancers, when an unfortunate button of his coat entangled itself in the lace of a lady's dress, and in the perturbation of his feelings he went down the middle and up again, carrying a long and tattered shred, that lengthened as he went. Fanny's was the dress – Fanny was the sufferer. But she looked up into his face so forgivingly, and her soft blue eyes so smilingly met his, and her rosy lips spoke his pardon in such sweet tones, that he mentally said, 'Dear, lovely Fanny, what an angel! What bliss to be loved by Fanny!' But when Florence stepped forward from among the dancers, with eager concern, her bright cheek flushed, her dark eyes sparkling, and her voice attuned to the gentlest tones of commiseration for the damage done to 'dear Fanny's dear love of a pretty dress' – when she gracefully begged her partner to excuse her, 'that she might pin up the dear love's tatters' – then, Mr Blorage felt very much inclined to repeat the above sentence over again, substituting the name of Florence for Fanny. Meantime, all eyes were attracted to the horrible dowager in the Chair of Truth. Had any Painter been present, he would have gone on his knees to beseech that dowager to sit to him for the personification of a Gorgon. Mr Blorage felt, after all, that he could no more dare to ask her a question than if she had been his Black Majesty from below, arrayed in gorgeous female attire. There she must sit, until kind Fate stepped in with three questions and released her. As he looked hopelessly towards the door, he saw the little piquante nose of Gatty Bland showing itself in good relief against a black coat near her. She had a little laced handkerchief tied under her chin; she went towards the dowager, changing the little laced kerchief into her hand; in her plain white dress she conveyed the dowager, all purple and gold, down the room, out at the door, and into the tea room. He blessed Gatty Bland mentally, and finished his dance with high credit to himself, and perfect satisfaction to the (in those parts) rather-difficult-to-please Lady Fitzcluck. As soon as he was free, he flew to seek a partner, either in Fanny the Fair or Florence the Beautiful.

They were together, and seemed almost alone. They were together – horror! – in the Chair of Truth; Fanny on the cushioned seat; Florence on the stuffed arm. Florence was still employed in pinning up the tatters of the torn dress of Fanny.

'What a beautiful picture; what a lovely contrast!' thought Dick, as he approached.

'There, Dear!' said Florence, with a remarkably emphatic stress upon the last word; 'I have pinned you up, and done the best I could for you, Dear. But I am glad to see, notwithstanding, that you are a monstrous figure, and not fit to look at, Dear.'

'Thank you, Florence, Dear!'

'Ah, you false thing! *I* see through your meekness and your affectation, as if you did not care about your dress. It is a pity Mr Blorage can't see you at home.'

'It's a pity Mr Blorage can't see *you* at home. Aunt longs for the day when she can rid herself of you: indolent, selfish, and useless creature that you are.'

'But Aunt comforts herself with the reflection that she has not such a firebrand in her house as *you* are. Aunt can well afford to put up with a little indolence where there is so much good temper.'

'It is better to be a little passionate than sulky, Love.'

'Is it, Love? Mr Blorage is the best judge of that. We have all our tempers, and you don't expect a perfect wife, do you, Mr Blorage?'

'I am very imperfect myself,' murmured the unfortunate Dick.

'Oh no, Mr Blorage,' cried Fanny and Florence together; 'You are everything that is nice and good tempered. And this is such a love of a house, that no one could be unhappy here.'

Here the duet ceased, and solos began.

'You would always be cross and fractious, Fanny,' said Florence.

'And you would always be rude and boisterous, Florence,' said Fanny.

'For you are a virago, and you know you are,' said Florence.

'For you are a hoyden,[54] and you know you are,' said Fanny.

'I am ashamed of you, my darling,' said Florence.

'I am disgusted with you, my precious,' said Fanny.

'Ladies, ladies!' expostulated Dick.

'She has the vilest temper, Mr Blorage!' cries Florence.

'She can't speak a word of truth, Mr Blorage,' cries Fanny.

As Mr Blorage turned hurriedly and appealingly from the one to the other, each now exclaiming, 'Throw your handkerchief to *me*, Mr Blorage!' he lost his balance, rolled over, and rolled the chair over.

Picking himself up with all possible despatch, and turning to apologise, he found that Florence, Fanny, music, lights, flowers, dancers, Lady Fitzcluck, and dowager, had all disappeared. There was nothing near him but *the* chair – overturned – and an empty wine bottle.

V

'Thank Heaven!' were the first spoken words of Mr Blorage. His first act was to look for his handkerchief, which he hoped he had not thrown to either of the ladies. It was safe in his pocket. 'It must have been a dream,' he next remarked, eyeing the chair dubiously. 'Yes, of course a dream,' as he gathered courage from its motionless state. 'But a very bad dream,' as he felt encouraged to touch it, raise it, and examine it. As harmless a chair as ever upholsterer stuffed, or gentleman bought! Gently he restored it to its proper place.

A knock at the door. Immediately followed by the appearance of the model Penge. It seemed an agreeable and satisfactory circumstance to the respectful Penge that his master was on his legs and awake.

'Shall I remove the things, sir? It's close upon nine.'

'Do so, Penge. And I think I will have a cup of coffee – rather strong, Penge.'

'Yes, sir.'

What a relief it was, not to see Penge sit down in the chair!

'It's a delicious cup of coffee, Penge,' said Mr Blorage, when it was brought, 'and it so perfectly agrees with me that I think I'll take a run over to Dr Evans' and play a game of chess with him.'

The sharp night air smote him with a sudden giddiness, and every twinkling star appeared to be closely embracing a twin star that twinkled with still greater vigour; but he soon got over these delusions, and before he reached Dr Evans' door was quite himself. On the way, however, he took himself seriously to task:

'How good of the night to be so fresh and fine, how kind of the pure stars to beam down on me so brightly, when I am a man full of evil and weak thoughts. I harboured a design against my fellow creatures of the basest sort; and, to add to my crime, it was directed against one whom I meant for a wife! True, I know nothing of Miss Fanny or Miss Florence, but the beauty of those two cousins, and a general sort of amiability that seems to belong to all girls. I'll make it my business to see more of both, and I'll try to be guided to a right choice at last.'

Mr Blorage was warmly welcomed by Dr Evans, who opened the door to him.

'Now this is friendly. I have had a very anxious case, which has caused me much worry these three days. It is happily past the crisis now, and I was just saying to my wife, how I should enjoy your stepping in.'

'I am heartily glad I came.'

'Of course you are. You are always kind and seasonable. When were you ever otherwise!'

The good Dick followed the doctor (who was a voluble and hearty doctor) up the stairs into the presence of Mrs Doctor. But Dick was unable to acknowledge Mrs Doctor's cordial greeting by so much as a single word; for there, before his eyes, seated on a little chair by Mrs Evans' side, was Miss Gatty Bland: her innocent little face peeping out of a handkerchief tied over her head and under her chin.

'You know dear little Gatty, of course?' remarked the Doctor. 'She is waiting for her mother's medicine. – I hope you have given Gatty a cup of tea, my dear?'

Mrs Doctor's face expressed a profound contempt for Mr Doctor's unnecessary reminder.

Meantime, Dick sat down. He awaited with the calm composure of a victim of Fate, for Miss Bland to offer him the use of her mother's beautiful china bowl.

She did nothing of the sort. In the ensuing half-hour she made no allusion whatever either to china or to bowls, though the conversation turned upon no other subject than his approaching house-warming.

Dick was half sorry. He felt as if it would be so agreeable to thank such a charming little girl. If her mother had lent him her china bowl (he felt sure she possessed a china bowl), he must have called to thank her; and he felt a desire to become intimate with the family. He might, perhaps, be of service to them; was there anything – or nothing – in that nomination he so nearly heard about? He invited Gatty to the house-warming, and anticipated her request for Jenny and Albert; he was not at all surprised to find that she *had* a sister Jenny and a brother Albert. But it did surprise him to see how pretty she became when joy flushed her cheeks and brightened her eyes, while several little dimples in the nicest corners of her face discovered themselves, as she smiled her thanks.

'The very thing!' said Mrs Evans; 'a little gaiety does more good than all my doctor's physic. Mr Blorage, my dear, very thoughtful. You'll expect all four, I dare say – three girls and a boy.'

'Only four! I expect eight at least.'

'But, Mrs Evans,' whispered Gatty, 'one of us must stay with mamma; that will be I, you know.'

'My dear, *I* will see to that. I will step down in the morning, Gatty, and settle it all with mamma.'

'And tell mamma from me,' said the doctor, 'that I shall spend a couple of hours with her tomorrow evening. I want to study her case, and I shall like a little rest between your dances, Blorage.'

'That is,' said Gatty, smiling delightedly, 'that you two are most kindly going to represent me for that time.'

'Just so, my dear. What! Are you off, Gatty? – Stay. We'll send our man, Mike, with you; the railway has brought a lot of ill-looking people about.'

'Let me take you home, Miss Bland,' said Dick.

'Oh! Thank you very much, Mr Blorage. I own some of the people frighten me, though I think they mean no harm.'

'We will have a game of chess when you come back, Blorage,' says the doctor.

What passed between little Gatty and her escort, and whether anything passed on the subject of china bowls, nobody knows. The walk did not last longer than ten minutes. My private opinion is, that Dick treated Gatty all the way with the respect and deference due to a young princess accidentally committed to his care. When he returned to his game of chess, what with the remaining fumes of that bottle of wine, the extraordinary dream, and this odd approach to an interpretation of it, it is certain that he was in a romantic mood. He willingly listened to a long history of the Blands, during which Mr and Mrs

Doctor maintained a laudatory duet very different indeed from the imaginary duet between Fanny and Florence.

'I only wish,' cried the doctor, at last, 'that I had a son of thirty, or thirty-five, with a good house, a good income, and a good heart. I would recommend him Gatty Bland for a wife with all my heart and soul, and he would thank me every year of his life ever afterwards, even though he had to marry her whole family along with her!'

'Miss Bland,' said Mr Blorage, 'spoke of a nomination – no, by the by, she didn't – it was a china bowl – dear me, what do I mean – I think I hardly know what I do mean!'

'You look rather wild, Dick; of course I can't help you out. *I* don't know what you discoursed upon in your walk; but there appears to me no affinity between a nomination for the Blue-coat School[55] and a china bowl.'

'Oh! that's what she wants, is it? Blue-coat School! God bless my soul! Really a nomination, eh? Blue coat! Ah! – Check to your queen!'

Notwithstanding that check, Dick lost the game. But he went home in a felicitous state of mind, which made him feel as if he had won the game. He continued to repeat the word 'Blue' to himself, as if he were under an obligation never to forget it; he went up to his bedroom, chuckling 'Blue!' he undressed, chuckling 'Blue;' he sat up in bed, after lying down, with a vehement 'Blue;' and his last recollection was a struggle to say 'Bluenomicoatation.'

VI

Mr Blorage arose in a contented and happy frame of mind. The great day was the greatest of successes; nothing marred the triumph of the dinner, nothing marred the beauty of the ball. The hard-faced dowager sat in *the* chair, but she was just as forcible and disagreeable as usual: no more and no less. Mr Blorage danced with Lady Fitzcluck, and bespoke Fanny, and Florence, and Gatty. For Gatty was there, demurely happy. Trust Mr and Mrs Doctor for Gatty's being there!

Florence looked most beautiful. She was charmingly dressed, in white tarlatan – three skirts – pinked – each skirt looped up with a mixture of white roses and pomegranate blossoms. A wreath of the same for her hair. Fanny was dressed in floating robes of blue – less blue than her eyes. Her fair curls were twined with silver leaves: she looked like a nymph; Florence like a queen. Not the greatest gossip in the room could say which was the favourite. Neither could the greatest, or the least, gossip in the room decide at what particular moment the star of both descended below Mr Blorage's horizon.

But he has confided to somebody, who confided it to me, who now confide it to you, that Miss Florence ceased to be beautiful in his eyes when she sneered at the plainness of the Miss Blands' muslin dresses. 'And it is real ivy in their hair, Mr Blorage, so they can't have gone to any great expense to do honour to your ball.' And Miss Florence glanced down at her own dress.

'I like them all the better for it,' stoutly answered Dick.

As to Miss Fanny, she was *so* astonished at the impertinence of such people as the Blands thrusting themselves into society so much above them! And her star descended, at the instant when she was thus overcome.

Mr Blorage accomplished his dances with Fanny and with Florence, but did not accomplish his dance with Gatty Bland. For on the instant that he claimed her hand, Dr Evans (sent off by his wife presently after dinner) returned from taking care of Mrs Bland.

'Oh! Mr Blorage, I must go – thank you so much for the happiest evening I ever spent, and the prettiest sight I ever saw!'

'No no no, you must not go; a quadrille takes only twenty minutes to dance.'

'But mamma is alone now, and I should be quite unhappy all that twenty minutes, even though dancing with you. But there is Jenny, she dances so well, and she loves it so much, and – don't think me conceited, Mr Blorage – she is so pretty.'

'She is the prettiest girl in the room – but one,' says Mr Blorage in a whisper. And as he assists Gatty to put on her cloak, he sees her, with unspeakable admiration, tie her little laced handkerchief over her head and under her chin, and look so indescribably like the dear darling little creature of his vision, that he longs – infamous as is (of course) the thought – to clasp her, then and there, to his heart! But instead of doing so, he flies back to the ballroom, and engages Jenny out of hand. Thus Gatty, when she went home, was able to tell her mother that she took a last peep at the beautiful scene, and saw kind Mr Blorage asking Jenny to dance, and Jenny looking as pretty as even those two lovely cousins Florence and Fanny. 'They say Mr Blorage is to marry one of them, mamma, but I hope not.'

'Oh, my Gatty!'

'Well, mamma, you know I see a good deal of them, here and there, and I am sure they are only pretty girls. They do not appreciate his great noble generous heart. But now, mamma, to bed you must go. No more excitement for you tonight.'

Happily, the excitement in the little family lasted a good many days, and afforded food for conversation, morning, noon, and night. Indeed, it was yet as fresh as ever, when, one morning, the post brought a piece of news that fairly surpassed the house-warming – a nomination to the Blue-coat School, in favour of no less a personage than Master Albert Bland. The commotion in that cottage – Well! It's a blessed thing to want something, for then you can duly appreciate the favour of having it. And it is a blessed thing to be rich, and liberal withal, for then you can bestow the favour so appreciated. Meantime, Mr Blorage divided his time pretty equally between his little office at the Bank, Dr Evans', the house belonging to the father of Florence, and the abode within which dwelt the lovely Fanny's aunt. And all these visits, combined with the still existing effects of his dream, ended in consequences.

The first consequence occurred to the self-satisfied William. His slow brother Dick acquired the ridiculous habit of demanding what Bill did with those sums of money he was forever borrowing? And – unkindest thing of all – Mr Richard insinuated, nay, he more than insinuated, he plainly told – Mr William Blorage that he expected such sums to be repaid in future. And to show that this was no idle threat, he produced a ledger, wherein a debtor and creditor account was drawn up between Mr Richard Blorage and Mr William Blorage: which account displayed a state of account so alarming to Mr William, that he reformed rather. Imagine Mr Dick's pleasure when William, Billy, or Bill, applied in sober seriousness for that post of junior of all the junior clerks, whilom[56] so despised by him!

Second important consequence. Mr Richard Blorage committed a piece of extravagance. He caused to be executed for himself, a statuette in white marble. Any orderers of statues, or other things to be made after a fashion of their own, may calculate what an enormous sum Mr Blorage paid for his statue. It must be ethereal-looking (he said), it must have extended wings, it must be lightly poised on one foot; but above all, it must have a slightly turned-up nose, and a little lace handkerchief tied under the chin!

* * *

These consequences came to pass ten years ago. On the night of the thirty-first of December, one thousand eight hundred and sixty-two, let us take a peep into Mr Blorage's house. Let us take a peep at Mr Blorage in his dining room. Dinner is over, wine and dessert are on table. The Chair is at the upper end of the room; above the chair, is a lovely statuette on a carved oaken bracket.

Dick is reading the paper; so, at the same time, is someone else. Dick holds the paper in his right hand; his left hand clasps a little tiny hand of the said someone else: while the matcher to that small hand of the same someone else turns the leaves of the paper, so that Dick feels he has no want of another hand. If the owner of the small hand gets to the bottom of the page first – which she invariably does, being a woman – she lays her head confidingly on Dick's shoulder, and seems very well content to let it stay there as long as Dick chooses.

But, hark! There is a noise overhead; a baize door closes with a muffled sound; there is a pattering of little feet, and there is a joyful chorus of little voices. Dick puts down the paper; his companion, flying to the door, opens it; in rush half a dozen small rosy boys and girls. (Most of these little children have noses of a slightly astronomical turn.)

Mamma prepares their dessert. There is a chair wanting at the table. In default of the missing chair, mamma wheels forward *the* Chair, and sits down in it.

'Papa, papa! Mamma is in the Chair of Truth,' cries a child.

Clearly Mr Blorage must have told his dream in the family circle.

'Then let us question her,' says papa. 'Mamma, are you happy?'

'Happy, as angels are said to be.'

'Do you love us?'

'As (under God) my chief good, my life.'

'Have you ever repented marrying Dick Blorage?'

This time the question is only answered by the surcharged eyes; expressive and loving eyes are often more ready to overflow from perfect happiness, than from distress or pain.

HIS WONDERFUL END
[by Charles Dickens]

It will have been, 'ere now, perceived that I sold the foregoing writings. From the fact of their being printed in these pages, the inference will, 'ere now, have been drawn by the reader (may I add the gentle reader?) that I sold them to One who never yet.*

Having parted with the writings on most satisfactory terms – for in opening negotiations with the present Journal, was I not placing myself in the hands of One of whom it may be said, in the words of Another† – I resumed my usual functions. But I too soon discovered that peace of mind had fled from a brow that, up to that time, Time had merely took the hair off, leaving an unruffled expanse within.

It were superfluous to veil it – the brow to which I allude, is my own.

Yes, over that brow, uneasiness gathered like the sable wing of the fabled bird, as – as no doubt will be easily identified by all right-minded individuals. If not, I am unable, on the spur of the moment, to enter into particulars of him. The reflection that the writings must now inevitably get into print, and that He might yet live and meet with them, sat like the Hag of Night[57] upon my jaded form. The elasticity of my spirits departed. Fruitless was the Bottle, whether Wine or Medicine. I had recourse to both, and the effect of both upon my system was witheringly lowering.

In this state of depression, into which I subsided when I first began to revolve what could I ever say if He – the unknown – was to appear in the Coffee Room and demand reparation, I one forenoon in this last November received a turn that appeared to be given me by the finger of Fate and Conscience, hand in hand. I was alone in the Coffee Room and had just poked the fire into a blaze, and was standing with my back to it, trying whether heat would penetrate with soothing influence to the Voice within, when a young man in a cap, of an intelligent countenance though requiring his hair cut, stood before me.

'Mr Christopher, the Head Waiter?'

'The same.'

---

* The remainder of this complimentary sentence editorially struck out.

† The remainder of this complimentary parenthesis editorially struck out.

The young man shook his hair out of his vision – which it impeded – took a packet from his breast, and, handing it over to me, said, with his eye (or did I dream?) fixed with a lambent meaning on me, 'THE PROOFS.'

Although I smelt my coat-tails singeing at the fire, I had not the power to withdraw them. The young man put the packet in my faltering grasp, and repeated – let me do him the justice to add, with civility:

'THE PROOFS. A. Y. R.'

With those words he departed.

A. Y. R.? And You Remember. Was that his meaning? At Your Risk. Were the letters short for *that* reminder? Anticipate Your Retribution. Did they stand for *that* warning? Outdacious Youth Repent? But no; for that, a O was happily wanting, and the vowel here was a A.

I opened the packet and found that its contents were the foregoing writings printed, just as the reader (may I add the discerning reader?) peruses them. In vain was the reassuring whisper – A. Y. R., All the Year Round – it could not cancel the Proofs. Too appropriate name. The Proofs of my having sold the Writings.

My wretchedness daily increased. I had not thought of the risk I ran, and the defying publicity I put my head into, until all was done, and all was in print. Give up the money to be off the bargain and prevent the publication, I could not. My family was down in the world, Christmas was coming on, a brother in the hospital and a sister in the rheumatics could not be entirely neglected. And it was not only ins in the family that had told on the resources of one unaided Waitering; outs were not wanting. A brother out of a situation, and another brother out of money to meet an acceptance, and another brother out of his mind, and another brother out at New York (not the same, though it might appear so), had really and truly brought me to a stand till I could turn myself round. I got worse and worse in my meditations, constantly reflecting 'The Proofs', and reflecting that when Christmas drew nearer, and the Proofs were published, there could be no safety from hour to hour but that He might confront me in the Coffee Room, and in the face of day and his country demand his rights.

The impressive and unlooked-for catastrophe towards which I dimly pointed the reader (shall I add, the highly intellectual reader?) in my first remarks, now rapidly approaches.

It was November still, but the last echoes of the Guy-Foxes[58] had long ceased to reverberate. We was slack – several joints under our average mark, and wine of course proportionate. So slack had we become at last, that Beds Nos. 26, 27, 28, and 31 having took their six o'clock dinners and dozed over their respective pints, had drove away in their respective Hansoms for their respective Night Mail-Trains, and left us empty.

I had took the evening paper to No. 6 table – which is warm and most to be preferred – and lost in the all-absorbing topics of the day, had dropped into a slumber. I was recalled to consciousness by the well-known intimation, 'Waiter!' and replying 'Sir!' found a gentleman standing at No. 4 table. The reader (shall I add, the observant reader?) will please to notice the locality of the gentleman – *at No. 4 table*.

He had one of the newfangled uncollapsable bags in his hand (which I am against, for I don't see why you shouldn't collapse, while you are about it, as your fathers collapsed before you), and he said:

'I want to dine, waiter. I shall sleep here tonight.'

'Very good, sir. What will you take for dinner, sir?'

'Soup, bit of codfish, oyster sauce, and the joint.'

'Thank you, sir.'

I rang the chambermaid's bell, and Mrs Pratchett marched in, according to custom, demurely carrying a lighted flat candle before her, as if she was one of a long public procession, all the other members of which was invisible.

In the meanwhile the gentleman had gone up to the mantelpiece, right in front of the fire, and had laid his forehead against the mantelpiece (which it is a low one, and brought him into the attitude of leapfrog), and had heaved a tremenjous sigh. His hair was long and lightish; and when he laid his forehead against the mantelpiece, his hair all fell in a dusty fluff together, over his eyes; and when he now turned round and lifted up his head again, it all fell in a dusty fluff together, over his ears. This give him a wild appearance, similar to a blasted heath.

'Oh! The chambermaid. Ah!' He was turning something in his mind. 'To be sure. Yes. I won't go upstairs now, if you will take my bag. It will be enough for the present to know my number. – Can you give me 24 B?'

(O Conscience, what a Adder art thou!)

Mrs Pratchett allotted him the room, and took his bag to it. He then went back before the fire, and fell a biting his nails.

'Waiter!' biting between the words, 'give me,' bite, 'pen and paper; and in five minutes,' bite, 'let me have, if you please,' bite, 'a,' bite, 'Messenger.'

Unmindful of his waning soup, he wrote and sent off six notes before he touched his dinner. Three were City; three West End. The City letters were to Cornhill, Ludgate-hill, and Farringdon-street. The West End letters were to Great Marlborough-street, New Burlington-street, and Piccadilly. Everybody was systematically denied at every one of the six places, and there was not a vestige of any answer. Our light porter whispered to me when he came back with that report, 'All Booksellers.'

But before then, he had cleared off his dinner, and his bottle of wine. He now – mark the concurrence with the document formerly given in full! – knocked a plate of biscuits off the table with his agitated elber (but without breakage) and demanded boiling brandy and water.

Now fully convinced that it was Himself, I perspired with the utmost freedom. When he became flushed with the heated stimulant referred to, he again demanded pen and paper, and passed the succeeding two hours in producing a manuscript, which he put in the fire when completed. He then went up to bed, attended by Mrs Pratchett. Mrs Pratchett (who was aware of my emotions) told me on coming down that she had noticed his eye rolling into every corner of the passages and staircase, as if in search of his Luggage, and that, looking back as she shut the door of 24 B, she perceived him with his coat already thrown off immersing himself bodily under the bedstead, like a chimley-sweep before the application of machinery.

The next day – I forbear the horrors of that night – was a very foggy day in our part of London, insomuch that it was necessary to light the Coffee Room gas. We was still alone, and no feverish words of mine can do justice to the fitfulness of his appearance as he sat at No. 4 table, increased by there being something wrong with the meter.

Having again ordered his dinner he went out, and was out for the best part of two hours. Enquiring on his return whether any of the answers had arrived, and receiving an unqualified negative, his instant call was for mulligatawny,[59] the cayenne pepper, and orange brandy.

Feeling that the mortal struggle was now at hand, I also felt that I must be equal to him, and with that view resolved that whatever he took, I would take. Behind my partition, but keeping my eye on him over the curtain, I therefore operated on Mulligatawny, Cayenne Pepper, and Orange Brandy. And at a later period of the day, when he again said 'Orange Brandy,' I said so too, in a lower tone, to George, my Second Lieutenant (my First was absent on leave), who acts between me and the bar.

Throughout that awful day, he walked about the Coffee Room continually. Often he came close up to my partition, and then his eye rolled within, too evidently in search of any signs of his Luggage. Half-past six came, and I laid his cloth. He ordered a bottle of old Brown. I likewise ordered a bottle of old Brown. He drank his. I drank mine (as nearly as my duties would permit) glass for glass against his. He topped with coffee and a small glass. I topped with coffee and a small glass. He dozed. I dozed. At last, 'Waiter!' – and he ordered his bill. The moment was now at hand when we two must be locked in the deadly grapple.

Swift as the arrow from the bow, I had formed my resolution; in other words, I had hammered it out between nine and nine. It was, that I would be the first to open up the subject with a full acknowledgement, and would offer any gradual settlement within my power. He paid his bill (doing what was right by attendance) with his eye rolling about him to the last, for any tokens of his Luggage. One only time our gaze then met, with the lustrous fixedness (I believe I am correct in imputing that character to it?) of the well-known Basilisk.[60] The decisive moment had arrived.

With a tolerable steady hand, though with humility, I laid The Proofs before him.

'Gracious Heavens!' he cries out, leaping up and catching hold of his hair. 'What's this! Print!'

'Sir,' I replied, in a calming voice, and bending forward, 'I humbly acknowledge to being the unfortunate cause of it. But I hope, sir, that when you have heard the circumstances explained, and the innocence of my intentions – '

To my amazement, I was stopped short by his catching me in both his arms, and pressing me to his breastbone; where I must confess to my face (and particular nose) having undergone some temporary vexation from his wearing his coat buttoned high up, and his buttons being uncommon hard.

'Ha, ha, ha!' he cries, releasing me with a wild laugh, and grasping my hand. 'What is your name, my Benefactor?'

'My name, sir' (I was crumpled, and puzzled to make him out), 'is Christopher; and I hope, sir, that as such when you've heard my ex – '

'In print!' he exclaims again, dashing the proofs over and over as if he was bathing in them. 'In print!! Oh, Christopher! Philanthropist! Nothing can recompense you – but what sum of money would be acceptable to you?'

I had drawn a step back from him, or I should have suffered from his buttons again.

'Sir, I assure you I have been already well paid, and – '

'No, no, Christopher! Don't talk like that! What sum of money would be acceptable to you, Christopher? Would you find twenty pounds acceptable, Christopher?'

However great my surprise, I naturally found words to say, 'Sir, I am not aware that the man was ever yet born without more than the average amount of water on the brain, as would *not* find twenty pound acceptable. But – extremely obliged to you, sir, I'm sure;' for he had tumbled it out of his purse and crammed it in my hand in two banknotes; 'but I could wish to know, sir, if not intruding, how I have merited this liberality?'

'Know then, my Christopher,' he says, 'that from boyhood's hour, I have unremittingly and unavailingly endeavoured to get into print. Know, Christopher, that all the Booksellers alive – and several dead – have refused to put me into print. Know, Christopher, that I have written unprinted Reams. But they shall be read to you, my friend and brother. You sometimes have a holiday.'

Seeing the great danger I was in, I had the presence of mind to answer, 'Never!' To make it more final, I added, 'Never! Not from the cradle to the grave.'

'Well,' says he, thinking no more about that, and chuckling at his proofs again. 'But I am in print! The first flight of ambition emanating from my father's lowly cot, is realised at length! The golden bowl'[61] – he was getting on – 'struck by the magic hand, has emitted a complete and perfect sound! When did this happen, my Christopher?'

'Which happen, sir?'

'This,' he held it out at arm's length to admire it, 'this Per-rint.'

When I had given him my detailed account of it, he grasped me by the hand again, and said:

'Dear Christopher, it should be gratifying to you to know that you are an instrument in the hands of Destiny. Because you *are*.'

A passing Something of a melancholy cast put it into my head to shake it, and to say: 'Perhaps we all are.'

'I don't mean that,' he answered; 'I don't take that wide range; I confine myself to the special case. Observe me well, my Christopher! Hopeless of getting rid, through any effort of my own, of any of the manuscripts among my Luggage – all of which, send them where I would, were always coming back to me – it is now some seven years since I left that Luggage here, on the desperate chance, either that the too too faithful manuscripts would come back to me no more, or that someone less accursed than I might give them to the world. You follow me, my Christopher?'

'Pretty well, sir.' I followed him so far as to judge that he had a weak head, and that the Orange the Boiling and Old Brown combined was beginning to tell. (The Old Brown being heady, is best adapted to seasoned cases.)

'Years elapsed, and those compositions slumbered in dust. At length, Destiny, choosing her agent from all mankind, sent You here, Christopher, and lo! the Casket was burst asunder, and the Giant was free!'

He made hay of his hair after he said this, and he stood a tiptoe.

'But,' he reminded himself in a state of great excitement, 'we must sit up all night, my Christopher. I must correct these Proofs for the press. Fill all the inkstands and bring me several new pens.'

He smeared himself and he smeared the Proofs, the night through, to that degree, that when Sol gave him warning to depart (in a four-wheeler), few could have said which was them, and which was him, and which was blots. His last instructions was, that I should instantly run and take his corrections to the office of the present Journal. I did so. They most likely will not appear in print, for I noticed a message being brought round from Beaufort Printing House while I was a throwing this concluding statement on paper, that the ole resources of that establishment was unable to make out what they meant. Upon which a certain gentleman in company, as I will not more particularly name – but of whom it will be sufficient to remark, standing on the broad basis of a wave-girt isle, that whether we regard him in the light of –* laughed, and put the corrections in the fire.

THE END OF THE CHRISTMAS NUMBER FOR 1862

---

* The remainder of this complimentary parenthesis editorially struck out.

NOTES

1. Large halls and inns where public gatherings and dinners were commonly hosted during this period.
2. The Old George IV Inn.
3. Neck handkerchief.
4. Established in 1859, Yorkshire Bank (later known as Yorkshire Penny Bank) was founded for the working classes with the intent of helping them to save their money.
5. Viscount Henry John Temple Palmerston (1784–1865), British Foreign Secretary from 1830 to 1841 and Prime Minister from 1855 to 1865.
6. The buildings used by the Association or College of Doctors of Civil Law in London, a society founded in 1509 to be responsible for civic law. The Probate Court took over its jurisdiction in 1857 and the buildings were ultimately destroyed.
7. Greedy, stingy, or penny-pinching people.
8. A workhouse or poorhouse (as opposed to a workers or trades union).
9. Etcetera.
10. Punning on A.1. and Avon, this is a reference to Act III.iii of Shakespeare's *Othello* (1604). Iago, planning to throw suspicion on Desdemona by planting her handkerchief in Cassio's room, says, 'I will in Cassio's lodging lose this napkin, / And let him find it. Trifles light as air / Are to the jealous confirmations strong… '
11. Calamanco, a woollen fabric with satin twill and checks on one side.
12. Staffordshire beer.
13. A fairy-tale villain who murdered his wives and kept them in a locked secret room.
14. 'Crown the hole' or 'crown the whole', an expression meaning 'to top it all off' or to complete something.
15. The red ribbon is a sign that Mutuel has received the medal of honour from the French Legion of Honour (*Ordre national de la Légion d'honneur*), an order of chivalry established by Napoleon.
16. From Thomas Dibdon's (1771–1841) poem, 'The Snug Little Island' (1833): 'Oh! what a snug little Island, / A right little, tight little Island! / All the globe round, none can be found / So happy as this little Island.'
17. A day for reviewing and evaluating military troops during their field exercises.
18. Marshal Vauban (1633–1707), Louis XIV's military engineer, responsible for fortifying almost all of the French border towns.
19. 'Damned' seems the most likely word for which Langley seeks a euphemism.
20. One who pretends to have certain knowledge in order to better his or her reputation; a fraud.
21. Probably the Saint Lawrence martyred in 258 of the Common Era for defending the poor.
22. Excessively well-groomed and adorned.
23. A variety of apple.
24. A reference to a German wine called Hochheimer and commonly used to refer to German white wine in general.

25. *Le prophète*, a popular nineteenth-century opera by Giacomo Meyerbeer, performed for the first time in London in 1849.

26. A French desert with sponge cake or bread (often ladyfingers) on the outside and custard or pudding on the inside.

27. A derogatory term for an effeminate man; also a person with some mastery of the fine arts.

28. Philip Astley (1742–1814) was a famous equestrian who ran a riding school in London and became well-known for pioneering circuses that featured acrobatic horse riding, or trick-riding.

29. To heave the log; to cast a reel and line into the water to which is fixed a small piece of wood (the log chip) in order to ascertain a ship's sailing speed.

30. A whist enthusiast immortalised in Charles Lamb's 1821 essay 'Mrs Battle's Opinions on Whist', which appeared in the February 1821 issue of *London Magazine*.

31. The highest deck on a large sailing vessel, positioned at the stern.

32. Fear.

33. A schooner or sailboat built in Nova Scotia.

34. Tin of pickled beef and soup.

35. The yard, or pole, to which the mainsail is attached.

36. Rest in peace (Latin).

37. Slang for food; often stockpiled provisions or rations.

38. Mount Rigi in Switzerland, known as the 'Queen of the Mountains'.

39. Food provisions, rations.

40. The protective raised woodwork that runs along the perimeter of a vessel above deck-level.

41. A pier in London's East End; in use through 1930, it was the main point of departure for most emigrants.

42. A walking or climbing stick.

43. The bow of a ship that faces the wind.

44. Lloyd's, a London association that provided marine insurance and also daily shipping information.

45. Baron Munchhausen: Karl Friedrich Hieronymus, Freiherr von Münchhausen (1720–97). A German baron famous for the tall tales he recounted of his adventures campaigning against the Turks. These stories were collected and published by numerous authors throughout the eighteenth and nineteenth centuries.

46. The line 'The world knows nothing of its greatest men' is spoken in Act I of the 1834 drama *Philip Van Artevelde* by Sir Henry Taylor (1800–86).

47. *The Stranger*, a popular sentimental melodrama translated from the German play *Menschenhass und Reue* (1789) by August F. F. von Kotzebue.

48. Minting or circulating forged money or coins.

49. Strangling with a wire, or otherwise assaulting a person, with the intention of robbing.

50. Something or someone noticeably abrasive or unkind.

51. The titular hero of Samuel Richardson's *The History of Sir Charles Grandison* (1753–4), an ideal gentleman who exhibited proper and decorous social form.

52. Consolidated Annuities; the government securities of England.

53. A reference to Mme de Genlis's story 'The Palace of Truth,' from her *Tales of the Castle; Or, Stories of Instruction and Delight*, first published in French in 1784 and translated into English in 1785 by Thomas Holcroft. 'The Palace of Truth,' the story of a Genii named Phanor who is given a palace in which no one is allowed to lie, suggests that lies facilitate sociable interaction.

54. A virago is an impertinent, assertive, and/or masculine woman; a hoyden is an impolite, bad-mannered woman.

55. A school funded by charitable donations and whose administrators and pupils wore blue coats or clothing.

56. At some time in the past.

57. Reference to the witches in Shakespeare's *Macbeth* II.iii: 'secret, black, and midnight hags!'

58. Celebrants of Guy Fawkes' Day (5 November 1605). Also known as the Gunpowder Plot, the Guy Fawkes incident was a failed attempt by Catholic extremists to kill King James I by blowing up the Houses of Parliament before the State Opening.

59. Literally 'pepper water', a spicy stew or soup of Indian origin.

60. A mythological monster with a serpent's tail and a deadly glance.

61. In *The Christmas Stories* (1996), Ruth Glancy notes that some later editions of *Somebody's Luggage* print 'golden bow.' However, it is also possible that the golden bowl is a somewhat awkward reference to Ecclesiastes 12:6 ('Remember him – before the silver cord is severed, / or the golden bowl is broken').

Charles Dickens (1812–70) was one of the Victorian period's most famous literary celebrities. Today, he is perhaps best known for his novels, many of which, such as *Oliver Twist* (1836–7), *David Copperfield* (1849–50), and *A Tale of Two Cities* (1859), have been adapted repeatedly for both the stage and screen. He was also a playwright, performer, and tremendously successful journalist who ran and edited two popular magazines aimed at middle- and lower-middle-class readers: *Household Words* (1850–9) and *All the Year Round* (1859–70). Between 1850 and 1867, Dickens devoted one journal issue per year to the subject of Christmas. Almost all of these Christmas stories were collaborative efforts, collections of stories commissioned and arranged by Dickens himself. He described this work not as editing so much as 'conducting' a narrative with friends and colleagues. *Somebody's Luggage* (1862) is one such 'conducted' Christmas tale from *All the Year Round*. Dickens eventually tired of these special Christmas issues and stopped producing them in 1868, but, in their heyday in the 1860s, they sold well into the quarter million range.

John Oxenford (1812–77) was a translator, playwright, and theatre critic for *The Times of London*. By the time of his death, he had written over 100 plays, including several successful farces and an extremely popular adaptation of Ellen Wood's novel *East Lynne* (1860), one of the longest-running melodramas on the British stage. As a translator, he produced well-received versions of Molière's *Tartuffe* (1664) as well as Goëthe's *Conversations with Goëthe* (1836). In 1857, Dickens invited Oxenford and several other theatre critics to the private performances of *The Frozen Deep*, the melodrama that Dickens had written with Wilkie Collins. Oxenford observed that Dickens, in the lead role of Richard Wardour, conveyed 'a strong irrational force' on stage that appealed to his audience.

Charles Allston Collins (1828–73) was the younger brother of popular novelist Wilkie Collins (1824–89), who was Dickens' friend and frequent collaborator. Charles produced three novels, *The Bar Sinister*

(1864), *Strathcairn* (1864), and *At the Bar* (1866). *At the Bar* was published in *All the Year Round*, to which he contributed regularly. These novels failed to earn much money, and today Collins is perhaps most remembered for his paintings, which featured the naturalistic style and religious themes favoured by the early Pre-Raphaelite Brotherhood. Collins married Dickens' third child and favourite daughter Kate (1839–1929) in 1860. Kate later claimed that she married Collins not out of love but as an excuse to escape her father's household, which had recently been thrown into domestic upheaval by Dickens' separation from his wife. Dickens disliked the frail and sickly Collins but permitted the match; the marriage lasted for thirteen unhappy years before Collins succumbed to stomach cancer.

Arthur Locker (1828–93) was both a novelist and prolific journalist who emigrated to Australia in 1852 in search of gold. His novels *Sweet Seventeen* (1866), *On a Coral Reef* (1869), and *Stephen Scudamore the Younger* (1871) all feature Australian settings. Ultimately unsuccessful in Australia, he returned to London in 1856, where he supported himself largely through his freelance journalism. He was eventually offered a permanent position as a staff writer at *The Times of London* and was later appointed chief editor of *The Graphic*.

Julia Cecilia Stretton, née Collinson (1812–78), began her writing career with children's books, which she produced as a means of supporting her family after her first husband died. Her first novel, *A Woman's Devotion*, was published in 1855. It and later novels, including *Margaret and her Bridesmaids* (1856), *Lords and Ladies* (1866), and *Three Wives* (1868), featured highly idealised Victorian heroines of virtue. *Margaret and her Bridesmaids* was especially popular in England, and was reviewed well on both sides of the Atlantic. The second daughter in a family of fifteen children, Stretton's books *The Valley of the Hundred Fires* (1860) and *The Queen of the County* (1864) draw heavily on her experience growing up in a large family; *The Valley of the Hundred Fires* contains a touching portrait of her parents. Stretton's social circle included Jane Welsh Carlyle (1801–66), who said upon their first meeting that Stretton 'captivated

[her] at first sight... There is a charm of perfect naturalness about her that is irresistible'.

Melissa Valiska Gregory received her PhD from Indiana University and is currently an Assistant Professor of English at the University of Toledo, where she specialises in nineteenth-century British literature. She has published scholarly articles on both Victorian poetry and the novel, and she is working on a book-length manuscript on narratives of domestic terror in Victorian culture.

Melisa Klimaszewski earned her PhD at the University of California, San Diego and is currently a Visiting Assistant Professor of English at Drury University, where she specialises in Victorian literature, World literature, and critical gender studies. She has published scholarly articles on nineteenth-century servants and is now pursuing a book-length project that focuses on Victorian nursemaids and wet nurses.

SELECTED TITLES FROM HESPERUS PRESS

Author	Title	Foreword writer
Dante Alighieri	*The Divine Comedy: Inferno*	Ian Thomson
Jane Austen	*Love and Friendship*	Fay Weldon
Charles Baudelaire	*On Wine and Hashish*	Margaret Drabble
Charlotte Brontë	*The Secret*	Salley Vickers
Anton Chekhov	*The Story of a Nobody*	Louis de Bernières
Wilkie Collins	*A Rogue's Life*	Peter Ackroyd
Joseph Conrad	*Heart of Darkness*	A.N. Wilson
Emily Dickinson	*The Single Hound*	Andrew Motion
Fyodor Dostoevsky	*Notes from the Underground*	Will Self
George Eliot	*Amos Barton*	Matthew Sweet
Gustave Flaubert	*November*	Nadine Gordimer
E.M. Forster	*Arctic Summer*	Anita Desai
Elizabeth Gaskell	*Lois the Witch*	Jenny Uglow
Johann Wolfgang von Goethe	*The Man of Fifty*	A.S. Byatt
Henry James	*In the Cage*	Libby Purves
John Keats	*Fugitive Poems*	Andrew Motion
Xavier de Maistre	*A Journey Around my Room*	Alain de Botton
Herman Melville	*The Enchanted Isles*	Margaret Drabble
Marcel Proust	*Pleasures and Days*	A.N. Wilson
François Rabelais	*Pantagruel*	Paul Bailey
Christina Rossetti	*Commonplace*	Andrew Motion
Marquis de Sade	*Betrayal*	John Burnside
Italo Svevo	*A Perfect Hoax*	Tim Parks
Leo Tolstoy	*Hadji Murat*	Colm Tóibín
Mark Twain	*The Diary of Adam and Eve*	John Updike
Virginia Woolf, Vanessa Bell with Thoby Stephen	*Hyde Park Gate News*	Hermione Lee